CHAPTER ONE
CHRISTMAS WITH AUNT JOANNA

"Who comes to a bed and breakfast for *Christmas*?" said Ruby Pilgrim, staring out of the windows in disgust.

"People who don't like cooking?" said Alex. He was busy hanging baubles on the enormous

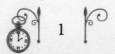

1

Christmas tree which stood in the hall at Applecott House. Their own tree at home had tinsel and knitted snowmen and all the decorations they'd made in nursery school, but this one was very classy – all colour-co-ordinated baubles and white lights. He secretly rather disapproved – he loved their messy, family tree – but he had to admit that Aunt Joanna's did look lovely.

"Christmas is for *family*!" said Ruby. "For spending all morning in your pyjamas eating selection boxes! You're supposed to spend it watching Christmas telly and playing video games and having fights over who does the washing up! Not going on holiday!"

"I don't think everyone spends Christmas

To my nephews and nieces,
McKenzie, Finlay
and Freya.

First published in the UK in 2020 by Nosy Crow Ltd

The Crow's Nest, 14 Baden Place
Crosby Row, London, SE1 1YW

Nosy Crow and associated logos are trademarks and/or registered
trademarks of Nosy Crow Ltd.

Text copyright © Sally Nicholls, 2020
Cover copyright © Isabelle Follath, 2020
Inside illustrations copyright © Rachael Dean, 2020

The right of Sally Nicholls to be identified as the author of this work
has been asserted.

ISBN: 978 1 78800 733 7

A CIP catalogue record for this book is available from the British Library.

Printed and bound in Great Britain by Clays Ltd, Elcograf S.p.A.

Papers used by Nosy Crow are made from wood grown in sustainable forests.

FSC
www.fsc.org

MIX
Paper from
responsible sources
FSC® C018072

1 3 5 7 9 10 8 6 4 2

www.nosycrow.com

playing video games and eating selection boxes," said Alex cautiously. "Not grown-ups anyway." He hung a very old-fashioned-looking reindeer on the tree, careful not to break it. *Some of these decorations are over a hundred years old*, Aunt Joanna had said to him. There had been Pilgrims living in Applecott House for over two hundred years. Had his father and his grandfather and all his great-great-grandparents hung some of those same baubles on their Christmas tree?

It was rather a nice thought.

Alex didn't need to imagine those people from another time – he'd met them; well, some of them anyway. Last summer, something mysterious and wonderful had happened to Alex and Ruby.

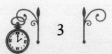

They'd stepped into a magical looking-glass in Aunt Joanna's hallway, and been transported back in time. They still didn't know why, but Alex believed they'd been sent there to help solve a historical problem – to find a lost Saxon treasure, and save Aunt Joanna's house in the process.

He had hoped that perhaps they were connected to the mirror now; that it would use them to right old-fashioned wrongs and solve ancient mysteries. Perhaps they would have a new adventure every time they came to stay with Aunt Joanna! But the problem was, they *didn't* come here very often. Applecott House was in Suffolk, and Alex and Ruby lived in a little town in the north east of England, two hundred miles and a long car journey away.

They came every summer, and often in the Easter holidays too, but when you've been sucked into a magical mirror and transported back to 1912 to solve a high-stakes crime, the Easter holidays is a very long time to wait to do it again.

And then, a week before Christmas, Aunt Joanna fell downstairs and broke her leg.

Christmas at Applecott House was the busiest time of year. Aunt Joanna organised a whole three-day celebration for her bed-and-breakfast guests, with a carol service in the village, a musical evening in the drawing room, and a Boxing Day quiz. There was fizzy wine with Christmas breakfast, and candlelit dinners on Christmas Eve and Christmas Day, which Aunt Joanna had

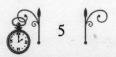

to cook. Alex privately agreed with Ruby that it didn't really sound like *Christmas* at all, but lots of grown-ups seemed to like it, and she was always booked out months in advance.

And now it looked like she would have to cancel.

Aunt Joanna had called the children's father in a panic. All of the food and wine was ordered already. She'd paid a deposit for the wine glasses and the musicians. Everyone was relying on her. She couldn't ask her own children to help (Aunt Joanna had a son who lived in Australia and a daughter who had baby twins, and obviously neither could be expected to drop everything and run Christmas in Applecott House). But perhaps Alex's family might be able to...

"There won't be any beds," said Alex's father. "All the rooms are booked, so we'll be sleeping in the living room, I'm afraid. Aunt Joanna thinks she should be able to supervise the cooking – at least I hope will, because you know what our cooking's like, and Stacey will be in as much as she can." Stacey was a woman from the village who helped Aunt Joanna out at busy times of year. "It's mostly getting the rooms ready ... and the washing up, and the vegetable-chopping ... and the decorations – apparently that's very important. And I suppose there'll be lots of tidying up and laying tables and so on. But she's been so good to us over the years – I don't know what we'd have done if she hadn't agreed to look after you

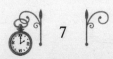

children. And… Well. I didn't really feel I could say no. And it's supposed to be rather a luxury holiday … I understand people pay a fortune, and of course we'd get to eat all the food and so forth. I think it might be quite fun, really…"

"But it's Christmas!" Ruby had said. "Christmas Day!"

"I don't imagine you children will have to help too much on Christmas Day itself," their mother said hurriedly. (Alex got the impression she wasn't keen on spending Christmas laying tables and loading dishwashers either.) "I expect you'll be able to hide somewhere with your presents if you'd rather."

"I don't see where," Ruby muttered. "We won't

even have a *bedroom*."

But Alex didn't really mind. Just being back at Applecott House – his favourite place in all the world – was enough to make him happy. They'd arrived yesterday, just after lunch, and even an afternoon spent making beds and vacuuming bedrooms had been fun. He'd enjoyed hanging up all the decorations, and helping Aunt Joanna ice Christmas biscuits. He was looking forward to eating all this fancy food – and after all, he thought, their father was right. Aunt Joanna was *family*.

"We're hardly going to see Mum and Dad all Christmas!" said Ruby furiously. "They're going to spend all day washing dishes and chopping

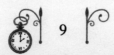

carrots, just you wait. It's going to be awful! I wish we were *anywhere* else. I wish we could just *leave* and go and have a *proper* Christmas. Anywhere!"

She swung away from the window to glare at Alex. And stiffened.

"Alex!"

"I know," said Alex, who'd seen it too. "I think you might be about to get your wish."

He hurried over to the wall, Ruby close on his heels. The mirror – the magic mirror, the time-travelling mirror, *their* mirror – now showed a middle-aged woman in a very old-fashioned dress – Victorian, probably, Alex thought – with a woollen shawl and big old-fashioned skirts. She was frowning at her reflection in the mirror, a hatpin

poised above her
hat. Then suddenly
something changed. A
look of astonishment
passed over her face,
as though she couldn't
believe what she was
seeing. She took a step
backwards, staring at
the mirror as though
it was a ghost.

"She can see us!" cried Ruby. She grabbed his
hand. "I didn't know that could happen."

The woman blinked, and rubbed her eyes. She
took a deep breath. And then slowly, cautiously,

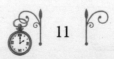

arm outstretched, she began to move towards the mirror.

"No!" Ruby cried. "If she touches it, she's going to come *here*. No way, old Victorian lady. This is *our* time-travelling adventure, not yours!"

She pulled Alex forwards, into the mirror …

…. and they landed on their hands and knees on the floor of the Victorian hallway.

The first thing that hit Alex was the cold. He'd known, in a vague sort of way, that the Victorians didn't have central heating, but he hadn't realised how *cold* that would make their houses. Victorians had fires, hadn't they? The Pilgrims weren't lords and ladies or anything like that, but they weren't exactly poor. The Edwardian Pilgrims had servants and things. But the hallway at Applecott House had no fireplace, and it was icy cold. Nearly as cold as being outside would be, Alex thought in dull horror. Was this really what Victorian houses were like?

Beside him, Ruby moaned,

"Oh no! Seriously? It's freezing! Summer! Can't we have summer?"

"You did ask for Christmas," Alex pointed out.

"I take it back! I want a heatwave! A heatwave!"

The woman was staring at them in understandable amazement. Alex wasn't great at grown-up ages, but she looked older than his mother and younger than Aunt Joanna. She was wearing a dark-blue dress, with a sticky-out bit

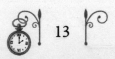

at the back, which Alex vaguely remembered was called a bustle (their parents liked costume dramas and telling their children useless bits of information). She had a green shawl around her shoulders, and greyish-brown hair done up in a bun with curly bits hanging out at the front. She had that look about her which Alex was beginning to recognise as *Pilgrim*, something inexplicable which marked her out as a friend and relation among the strangers of the past. Alex wasn't sure exactly what it was, but it was something energetic, something cheerful, something that looked on the world as a game to be played or a treasure chest to be opened and explored. Even his funny, awkward, serious father had it, even *Ruby* did, though she sometimes pretended she didn't. Alex had never heard the phrase *intellectual curiosity*, but he would have understood it immediately; a sort of interest and enthusiasm for the world and all its doings. Alex knew without being told that he was related to this woman, that she would be pleased and excited to see him, and that once she'd recovered from her astonishment, they would be safe with her.

He wasn't prepared for what she actually said, which was: "Alex and Ruby! It *is* you, isn't it?"

15

CHAPTER TWO
CHRISTMAS
IN 1872

For a moment, all they could do was stare. Then Ruby said, "Do we *know* you?"

"Why, yes! At least – I know you. And you *will* know me – or you did – or you're going to –" She stopped in confusion, then laughed. "Great

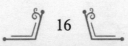

heavens, time travel is a most peculiar thing, is it not? I declare, one needs a whole new dictionary!"

"I'm lost," said Alex.

"I'm not," said Ruby slowly. "I *think* what she means is, we're going to meet her in an adventure we haven't had yet. Sometime in *our* future, we're going to go back to *her* past – that's right, isn't it?"

"Indeed it is." The woman beamed at her and held out a hand. "Marian Pilgrim – Marian Barnes as was. Last time I saw you, I was eleven years old. Many a long day I've waited to see you again. I'd almost got to the point of believing the whole affair was a childish fancy – and here you are!"

Here they were. Alex looked slowly around the

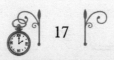

hallway. He'd always thought clutter was a modern thing, but this hallway was full of way more stuff than Aunt Joanna's. There was a row of pegs against the wall, full of enough cloaks and coats to clothe a whole classful of children. Below them were an untidy collection of boots and rubber overshoes and umbrellas and walking sticks, not to mention several metal hoops, two cricket bats and some stumps, a few mouldy-looking balls, a dog's lead, and what looked like a whip. Below the pegs was a table, covered in bits of paper and newspapers and brown-paper parcels and handkerchiefs and gloves and all the other detritus of family life. A pile of books and a heap of children's toys spilled over on to the floor, where an entire box of lead soldiers had been emptied out and abandoned next to someone's bag. Hung up on strings around the room were Christmas cards, just as they were in Aunt Joanna's hallway, though these were smaller and duller, and decorated with pictures of angels and robins and Victorian children.

It was also *dark*. The hallway was lit with what he supposed must be gaslights: actual yellow flames in little brass sconces against the walls. The light of the flames was much dimmer than an electric light. It gave the whole place a strange, rather mysterious air to it; something of the feel of a haunted house, only friendlier.

Above their heads, they could hear children's voices yelling, a dog yapping, and someone

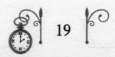

thumping away on a piano. From the kitchen came the sound of a woman singing *God Rest You Merry Gentlemen* in a strong Suffolk accent. The hall smelt of frost and coal-smoke and tobacco and cake cooking somewhere nearby. Despite the cold, Alex could feel himself starting to grin.

"It's Christmas, isn't it?" he said. "It's a Victorian Christmas! Isn't it?"

"Victorian?" said Marian. "Oh, yes, I see! After the Queen! How jolly! Yes, naturally you do not know where – or should I say when? – you are. Let me see – it is 1872, and tomorrow is Christmas Eve. This is Applecott House – but you know that, of course – and I live here with my husband, Charles, who is the village doctor. We shall have a full house for Christmas – my harum-scarum lot: five children still at home, Heaven help me. I hope you don't mind a bit of high spirits, for there'll be plenty of that, I assure you. Then there's my husband's brother, Elijah, and his little girl, over from India." Marian pulled a face as she said *Elijah*, and Alex got the distinct impression she didn't like him. "And tomorrow we'll have my eldest and his family, and my mother as well! And you," she added, almost as an afterthought.

"Will we fit?" said Ruby.

Marian grinned. "Come now! As though I'd turn away time-travellers at Christmas. We must hurry though, for if you are to be Christmas guests, it would never do for the servants to see you dressed

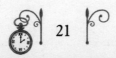

21

like this. Come!"

She made little shooing gestures at them and, rather bewildered, Alex and Ruby let her lead them up the stairs, and into another, even more cluttered, box room. This was evidently a storeroom, as most of the floor was covered in suitcases, trunks, and packing cases filled with oddments.

"There!" Marian sat back and looked at them with satisfaction. "We shall be safe from prying eyes here. And now – if my memory serves, you are sent into the past to right wrongs, are you not? So to what purpose have you been sent here?"

"How should we know?" said Ruby. "Don't you?"

"I have not the first idea," said Marian promptly. "I would say we are pretty jolly sorts, all told. But, there! Perhaps there is a tiger on the loose and we do not know it. I beg you, when you have discovered your task, tell me instantly, and I shall do all I can to assist you."

"I tell you what you could do to assist," said Ruby. "Can you think of a story to explain who we are and why we're here?

"Why, yes... Ah! I have it! You shall be the children of a poor schoolfellow of mine, newly returned to the country from ... now, where shall you hail from? America? Australia? Peru?"

"America," said Alex quickly. He didn't think he'd be able to pretend to have come from

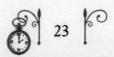

Victorian Peru.

"America it shall be! And my poor dear schoolfellow, sadly fallen gravely ill just before Christmas, knowing nobody hereabouts, puts you both into a stagecoach and dispatches you to me. How does that sound?"

"Will they believe it?" said Ruby.

Marian laughed. "It matters little if they do not, for this is my house, and I may invite who I please for Christmas. The children will be glad to have more playfellows, for I am sorry to say they find their cousin Edith rather dull company. And naturally I shall tell my husband the truth. He is a great believer in magic of all kinds, and besides, he has met you before, though I wager he will not remember."

Alex felt a little bewildered. Twenty minutes ago, he'd been hanging baubles on Aunt Joanna's Christmas tree, and now he was supposed to be an American Victorian (were Americans Victorian as well, or was that just British people?), fresh from his mother's sickbed. It was rather a lot to take in all at once. Still, he couldn't help liking Marian. And it was nice to think that there would be a grown-up looking after them on this adventure. Even if she did seem to do everything at about a hundred miles an hour.

"And now!" she was saying. "We must find you something more suitable to wear. I believe I have some clothes of Anne's put aside for Aquila, which

should do you very well, my dear." This was to Ruby. "And some outgrown things of Harold's which I fancy he will not remember. Come! For you must dress as we do if our story is to be a success."

There was a large wooden chest at the foot of the bed. Marian opened it and began pulling out clothes any old how and piling them on the bed.

"Let me see... I am sure we have something in here somewhere, that... Aha! And this! And I believe these will do very well for dinner. There!"

She beamed at them. "Who is to go first?"

"Me," said Ruby. "This house is *freezing*. I want all the Victorian underwear you can throw at me. And fast!"

Ruby's suspicion was right. There was a *lot* of Victorian underwear. First, there was a chemise: a sort of white cotton tube which came down to her knees. Then, drawers. These were also very simple: two woollen tube legs attached to a waistband, like very baggy short trousers.

"But they don't..." Ruby blushed, then managed, "But they don't have any middle!"

They didn't. They kept the legs warm, but there was a bare space in the middle – perhaps to let Ruby go to the toilet?

"Why, no." Marian looked surprised. "Why should they?"

"Well, don't you ... I mean, what about when you're..." She stopped in confusion. "I thought

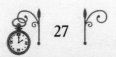

covering your bits up was the whole point of knickers!" she burst out at last.

"Indeed it is." Marian's face showed nothing but vague confusion. "It wouldn't do for a young man to see your legs."

"That isn't what I meant at all!" said Ruby.

"To be fair," said Alex, interested despite himself. "Why *do* you need … er … the rest of you covered up? I mean, I can understand if you're wearing jeans or something, but you don't really need pants when you're wearing skirts, do you? Why do people wear them at all?"

"I …" Ruby had gone bright scarlet. "Let's just change the subject, OK?"

Black woollen stockings were next. (Marian's

stockings, Alex noticed with interest, were pale green.) The stockings were like tights, but they stopped just above the knee and were kept up with a strap called a garter. Then a corset. Alex had heard about corsets; girls wore them to give themselves tiny waists, and they were supposed to be very tight and awful. They had strings at the back which someone had to pull and then tie to keep the girl's body stuffed in. Ruby looked at hers with active dislike.

"Do I *have* to?" she said.

"Yes, indeed." Marian looked shocked. "It's frightfully bad for your internal organs to be unsupported, you know. Why, it causes all sorts of internal problems."

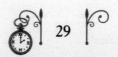

"Boys seem to manage all right," said Ruby.

"Well, boys are different," Marian said firmly. "Come now, don't be a goose. A great girl like you minding a little thing like a corset!"

She helped Ruby into the corset and tightened the strings at the back. Alex watched, fascinated. It wasn't just that Ruby's waist shrunk, her breasts – such as they were – were pushed upwards, giving her something like an actual cleavage.

"How do you feel?" he asked.

"Stiff," she said. "I can't bend! And everything's sort of *squashed*." She considered for a moment. "It's not as bad as I thought it was going to be, though. I thought girls were always fainting and so forth because they were stuffed into corsets."

"Fainting!" Marian laughed. "My dear, the servants work twelve-hour days, cooking and cleaning and fetching and carrying, all in corsets. If they're as unhealthy as all that, how in heaven's name do you think they manage?"

"I never really thought," Ruby admitted.

"I don't say," Marian went on, "that in fashionable circles, girls never indulge in a little … over-tightening. Some of their so-called fashionable waistlines – well! I wouldn't say I approve of *that*. But I don't know where a young girl would be without a nice, sensible supported midriff."

"Huh!" said Ruby.

Above the corset came the petticoats: one cotton, one flannel.

"Don't they feel weird?" said Alex, watching Ruby as she took an experimental walk across the room.

"Very," she said. "I wouldn't like to run in them. They're warm, though. I bet you'll wish you had petticoats after a couple of days in a house like this."

Over the petticoats went a thick knee-length dress in dark red. Since it was nearly dinner time, Marian said they might as well dress for dinner – apparently everyone had to put on different clothes in the evening, Alex wasn't sure why. Ruby also had a slightly plainer dress and a white apron for daytime wear. Alex grinned when Ruby tried it on.

"You look like Alice in Wonderland!" he said.

"Alice Through the Looking-Glass you mean," said Ruby. She grinned back. "Hey, at least it's got pockets! More than you can say for modern girls' clothes!"

Last came a pair of black slipper-type shoes, which looked (Alex thought secretly) not that different to Ruby's twenty-first-century school shoes. There were also a pair of black ankle boots for outside. These fastened with a whole length of little black buttons, which had to be done up with a button-hook.

"Seriously?" Ruby said, but Alex could see she was secretly rather pleased. He would have rather liked the chance to have a go with the button hook

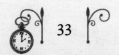

himself.

Alice in Wonderland had worn her hair loose, but Marian took a hairbrush and plaited Ruby's into two pigtails, which she tied up with lengths of ribbon.

"You'll want it out the way, if you're going to spend Christmas with my rowdy lot," she said. She stood back and looked at Ruby with evident satisfaction. "There! And there's a shawl in case you get cold. Now, don't you look smart!"

Alex's clothes were simpler. First there was a woollen vest – well, Marian called it a vest, but it had long sleeves that came all the way to his wrists. Then drawers, also wool, which came most of the way down his legs. Then a shirt, with a stiff

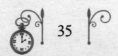

detachable collar and cuffs, and what Marian called a "Norfolk", which turned out to be a pair of tweed knickerbockers and a tweed jacket. These were thick, and wonderfully warm. Like Ruby, he was expected to wear black stockings and garters and black indoor shoes.

"Bet you aren't as warm as me, though," said Ruby, watching all this with interest.

To complete the outfit, they were both issued with a clean white pocket handkerchief.

"There!" said Marian. She looked at them with satisfaction, and beamed. "Now! Come and meet the rest of the horde."

CHAPTER THREE
A HORDE
OF PILGRIMS

"They're in the schoolroom," Marian said, over her shoulder. "At least – the younger ones are. Latimer's my eldest; he's twenty-two, if you can believe it! He's married, with a baby of his own; they'll be coming tomorrow. And Anne's

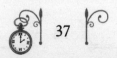

downstairs; she's seventeen, so hardly a child either. But the others are all here. You'll find them a jolly lot, I fancy."

They were certainly noisy. The schoolroom was a confusing whirl of black stockings and knickerbockers and red cheeks and shouting. The younger children had built a fort out of chairs and cushions and lengths of what looked like curtain fabric. An older boy, about fourteen, was sitting on an old armchair with his feet on the seat and his bum on the backrest. He was smoking a pipe, reading a very battered-looking copy of *The Adventures of Roderick Random* and shouting occasional instructions to the younger children, who ignored him. A little black-and-white terrier-type dog was leaping about around the younger children's feet, barking furiously.

Then there were two younger boys; one about Alex's age who was dressed in what looked like an actual pirate's hat, with a red-and-white-spotted handkerchief tied around his neck. The hat was adult-sized and kept slipping over his eyes. He was waving a wooden sword around and bellowing. Alex was rather taken aback; kids in his school had definitely grown out of pretending to be pirates, but this boy didn't seem to have at all. There was a much smaller boy, who looked about six and was busy clambering up the pile of chairs and yelling, "Avast, you scurvy sea-dog!" So perhaps the chairs were a pirate ship, not a fort.

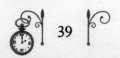

There were also two girls. One looked about nine, with a great mane of thick black hair, which swung about her face as she hopped and howled around the fort. She was brandishing a wooden sword, waving a battered wooden shield, and wearing an upturned pudding basin on her head.

Standing at the edge of the room, and watching all this with an expression of horror, was a little girl who must be cousin Edith from India. While the other children had rosy cheeks and thick, shiny hair in various shades from black to brown, Edith was small and white-faced and thin, with flat, dull fair hair and a sharp, narrow face. She was standing rather stiffly, dressed all in black: black dress, black shoes, black stockings. Even

her hair-ribbons were black. She was not dressed up. She was not playing. She looked as though she'd rather be anywhere but there.

"That's Edith," said Marian in a low voice, seeing his gaze. "Her mother died, poor soul, and her father's brought her over to England to be educated. She's going to go to boarding school in Ipswich, poor little wretch."

"Boarding school?" said Ruby. "How old is she?" Edith looked about six.

"She's eight," said Marian. "It's what everyone does, and I confess it doesn't seem to hurt the children … but it hardly seems right, does it? A little scrap like that. I had hoped she might come to us for the holidays at least, but Elijah wouldn't think of it. I'm sorry to say he's never approved of our madcap household."

"She's going to stay at boarding school *in the holidays*?" Ruby looked appalled. She'd also spoken louder than she realised. The children playing pirates looked round and saw them standing there.

"Mother!" cried the littlest boy, swinging his sword in delight.

"What ho!" said the boy with the pipe, nodding at them. "What's this, Mother? New comrades?"

"That's right," said Marian. "And I hope you're going to behave like civilised creatures, as they're going to stay with us for Christmas. This is Ruby and this is Alex. Their mother is a dear friend of

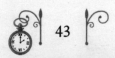

mine who is very ill, and they have nowhere else to go, so you must all be friends, for my sake and hers."

The children looked at Alex and Ruby with frank interest. The oldest boy waggled his eyebrows at Alex, who found himself grinning. He couldn't help it. They all looked so friendly and happy and … well … like family.

"Pleasure to meet you!" the eldest boy said. "I'm Harold – I'm the captain now, since Latimer married, and Anne is far too grown-up for us these days. It's a terrible trial when one's relations decide to grow up, but I suppose the alternative's worse."

"And I'm Wallace," said the next boy, the one

who looked about Alex's age. "Like William Wallace, but we're not Scots or anything like it. I'm named after a distant relation Mother hoped might sling me some cash – but all I got was a silver Christening ring, worst luck."

"Really, Wallace!" said Marian.

"And the dog is Bunyan," Wallace said with a grin. "He's supposed to be everyone's, but he's mine really. You know how dogs are. I trained him from a pup and all that. Bunyan, sit! Look here, sit, can't you?"

"Bunion?" said Alex. He wasn't *exactly* sure what a bunion was, but he thought it was rather like a verruca.

"Yes, because we're Pilgrims, don't you see?"

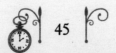

said Wallace, leaving Alex completely baffled.

"And I'm Aquila," said the girl with the black hair. "If you won't let me play, you'll be hung, drawn and quartered by sunset!"

"Aquila …" said Marian, but she sounded rather amused than otherwise.

"I'm Noel," said the littlest boy, hopping up and down. "I'm six and a half. And I'm ever so sorry about your mother. I do hope you'll have a happy Christmas anyway, and she doesn't die."

"Really, Noel!" said Marian, and Alex said hurriedly, "Oh no, she's not going to die. She's going to be fine."

"And *that* there's Edith," said Aquila. "She's rather awful, but she's only our cousin, so don't blame *us*."

At this last, Marian, who had been listening to her offsprings' remarks with a mixture of amusement and resignation, suddenly showed a different face. Grabbing Aquila by the arm, she pulled her forward.

"Now, that is *enough*. I mean it! A great girl like you, and you can't even be polite to a guest. I've a good mind to take all your Christmas presents away and give them to Edith, and if you carry on like this, I *will*. You are to apologise *this instant*, and you are *never* to say anything like that to a guest in this household again. *Do I make myself clear?*"

Aquila scowled and scuffed the floor with her

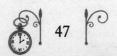

foot, but she muttered, "I 'pologise," in the vague direction of Edith.

Little Edith clenched her fists. She stuck out her chin, then she pushed Aquila so hard that Aquila toppled backwards with an "Oh!" and landed on the floor.

Then she turned and ran out of the door, slamming it behind her.

There was a stunned pause.

"Oh dear!" said Marian. "I suppose – oh, Aquila, don't *fuss* so, you're quite all right. I suppose I better *had* go after her…"

She hurried out of the door.

Aquila said furiously, "That little *beast*!"

"Well, you did deserve it," said Harold. "Don't

squawk, you know you did. And it must be pretty rotten to be her … that awful father … and her mother's dead … and now he's going back to India and she's to be dumped in school until she's grown up. No wonder she's miserable."

"Golly," said Wallace. "I'd simply love to go to school. I'm going to Harold's school when I'm fourteen, and they have such larks! No parents, lots of games … all those other chaps. I wish Mother would send us now. A fellow *does* get tired of his brothers and sisters sometimes."

"Don't you go to school at all?" said Alex.

Wallace shook his head. "We have lessons with Mr Thomas in the village – he's the curate, you know. He's a decent sort, I don't say he isn't. And

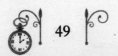

I must say, if I had a kid as small as that one, I'd let her live here with us. Mother would look after her, and Scotsborough always struck me as a beastly sort of place."

"Scotsborough!" Ruby opened her eyes wide at Alex in horror, and he could see her trying to telegraph something to him, though he wasn't sure what. "That's where she's going? Scotsborough in Ipswich? The charity school? *Why?*"

And then he realised. They'd been to Scotsborough – their parents had taken them there on an Educational Day Trip, of the sort parents were fond of. There had been a room done out to look like a Victorian schoolroom, and another laid out like a dormitory. There had been a kitchen, and a yard, and copies of children's workbooks and samplers. And lots of display boards with information about the school.

It had sounded a terrible sort of place. Children were fed gruel – a sort of very weak porridge, apparently – and not nearly enough food. They'd been whipped – there were real canes in some of the display cases. And lots of the children had actually died. The school had had regular epidemics of dreadful diseases (he thought cholera had been one, but he wasn't sure – it might have been typhoid or scarlet fever. Something awful and deadly and Victorian, anyway). There was a graveyard next to the school, full of the bodies of tiny Victorian schoolchildren.

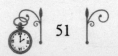

"I don't think it's a charity school exactly," said Harold doubtfully. "And it isn't at all the thing for English children to stay in India. They never do. There aren't the schools—"

"Yes, yes," said Ruby impatiently. "I've read *A Little Princess*. I know all that. But, listen, *Scotsborough*. Honestly—"

They were interrupted by the sound of a gong from downstairs.

"Dinner!" said Aquila. "Come on! Who cares what happens to beastly old Edith?"

She headed for the door, and the others followed. Ruby caught hold of Alex's sleeve and dragged him backwards.

"Scotsborough!" she said, as soon as the others

were ahead of them on the stairs.

"Yes, yes, I know," he said.

But she was shaking her head. "February 1873! That was when there was that big cholera epidemic – don't you remember? Two-thirds of the children died. I know it was then because there was this big memorial plaque outside the school with big scary angels on it, and I had it as my screen-saver on my phone for ages, because it was all cool and Gothic and creepy and – what?"

"Nothing," said Alex. *Trust Ruby*, he thought.

"Anyway!" said Ruby. "Two-thirds of the children! I bet that would include Edith, don't you? She's hardly blooming with health *now*, and that's before she's even got there. Don't you see?

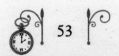

This is what we have to do! We've got to persuade that father of hers to send her somewhere else. Or she'll *die*."

"*Maybe* die," said Alex. "And why would her father listen to us?"

Ruby clenched her jaw. "I'll *make* him listen," she said. "No father would want to send their child to a school where two thirds of the pupils *die*, would he? Not unless he's actually evil. He's a Pilgrim, isn't he? He must not know – how could he, if he's only just come back from India? He probably just read the prospectus and thought it looked good, and I bet they never mentioned mass illness and death, did they? So we'll tell him. And then he'll change his mind and send Edith somewhere else, and we can all go back to somewhere with central heating for Christmas. Simple!"

"Hmm," said Alex. He wasn't sure it would be quite so easy.

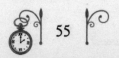

CHAPTER FOUR
VICTORIAN
PLUMBING

Dinner was downstairs, in the dining room. Noel
and Edith and Aquila had already eaten; nursery
tea in the schoolroom, boiled egg, soldiers and rice
pudding. They were hustled off by Noel's nanny
to get ready for bed. The older children, however,

were considered old enough to dine downstairs.

Somehow, Alex had expected something very formal; candlesticks and lots of courses and maybe a butler. It wasn't *very* much like that, though the food *was* brought in by a maid – at least, he supposed she was a maid, though she didn't wear a black-and-white uniform like maids on television. Just a rather shabbier version of Marian's dress. The food was what their mother called "stodge"; a big mutton joint swimming in gravy, and potatoes, and a few stringy over-boiled vegetables. It was the sort of food Ruby usually turned her nose up as "disgusting school dinner muck", but she ate it all and even asked for more. So did Alex. The house was so cold, he couldn't

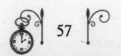

see how anyone could possibly want stir fry and salad and healthy stuff like that. (Even if they *liked* stir fry and salad, which Alex didn't.) There was a fire in the dining room, so it was warmer than the school room, but still much, much colder than the twenty-first century, even in all their Victorian layers. You wanted something warming. After the mutton, they had suet pudding with custard.

The meal was a cheerful, noisy affair. The little dog sat at Wallace's feet, eating anything which fell off their plates, or was passed to him.

"Wallace, don't! I shall send that dog down to the kitchen, I really shall," said Marian, but nobody paid any attention.

The Pilgrim children all talked loudly at the

tops of their voices, and so did Marian and the children's father, who was a doctor. (Alex and Ruby had to call him Dr Pilgrim, and Marian Mrs Pilgrim. Grown-ups never had first names in the past.) He was a cheerful, red-faced man with fantastic gingery whiskers, who rushed in just as the meal was starting.

"What ho!" he said. "Sorry I'm late everyone – triplets just been born up in Lower Bridges. Oh!" – as he caught sight of Alex and Ruby – "Did I forget you were here, or are you new?"

"Ruby and Alex," said Marian hurriedly. "They are staying for Christmas. I'll explain later." She turned to Alex and Ruby. "This is my husband, dears. He's really very competent, despite

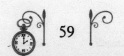

appearances. *Do* sit down and eat before it gets cold, darling."

And Dr Pilgrim sat, amid a chorus of enthusiastic questions about the new-born triplets and suggestions for appropriately Christmassy names.

There was also Anne, the children's older sister, a cheerful young woman with her hair up in a bun and long skirts.

"Goodness, Mother!" she said, when she saw Alex and Ruby. "More brats for Christmas! Where in heaven's name are they going to sleep?"

"In your bed if you keep behaving like that," Marian said. "What did I ever do to produce such unmannerly infants?"

"Hospitality is a Christian virtue," murmured

Uncle Elijah. The children stared at him, then Anne laughed.

"There you go, Mother!" she said. "You aren't being lunatic, you're being Christian!"

Uncle Elijah sipped his soup and looked disapproving.

He was about as different as could possibly be imagined from his brother. He was thin – painfully so – and, despite coming from India, very pale. Like Edith, he was dressed entirely in black (Victorians did that when people died, Alex remembered, and of course, his wife *had* died). But perhaps in his case it was also because he was a vicar? He was an army chaplain, that was why he was in India. He was wearing a little white dog-

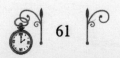

collar, just like modern vicars did.

Looking at him, Alex could see why the children didn't like him. He had a face that looked like he'd bitten down on a cake and had it turn into a lemon. His mouth turned downwards, and his eyes were cold and disapproving. Despite Marian's best efforts to be cheerful and friendly, he said very little, answering each question he was asked with a "Yes," or a "No," or an "Indeed."

And once, when Harold and Wallace were squabbling over the last bit of gravy in the gravy-boat, he lifted his cold eyes and said, "Children should be seen and not heard."

"Children!" said Harold. "I like that!"

It seemed impossible that someone so awful-looking could be related to the rest of the noisy family. But apparently he was.

After dinner, the women and children were supposed to go to the drawing room, while the children's father and Elijah got to stay and drink port and smoke cigars.

Elijah, however, had other ideas.

"Cigars are the devil's work, brother," he said. "And wine is a poison and a corrupter of virtue." And he rose with great dignity, as the women had.

"Ah well," said Charles. "I shall join you when the devil and I have finished our cigars." And he raised his glass.

The others all filed out and into the drawing

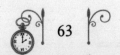

room. Anne sat down by the fire and pulled out some embroidery, Marian had a pile of mending, Harold a book, and Wallace said, "Anyone for cards?" with an eager glance at Alex and Ruby.

Alex and Ruby looked at each other.

"Yes, all right –" said Alex.

"Only there's something we have to do first," said Ruby, firmly.

Elijah was lingering by the magic mirror, fussing with his hair. Alex wondered what on earth they were doing, but Ruby marched straight over to him.

"We've got to tell you something," she said. "It's important."

He looked at her in some astonishment. "I really

don't think—"

"It's about Scotsborough, that school you're going to send Edith to. It's an awful place. They have cholera epidemics, and typhoid and … and all sorts. They don't feed the children. They don't have proper heating. It's child neglect! You can't send Edith there."

"Oh indeed?" said Elijah. There was an undertone of menace to his voice.

"Let her stay here," said Ruby at once. "It would be free! And she'd have a proper family and could do lessons here like the other children do. Marian – I mean, Mrs Pilgrim – she wouldn't mind. It's the perfect solution! And—"

But whatever else Ruby was about to say

was interrupted by a scuffling from the landing above, and a noise like muffled giggles. Then someone cried, "Go!" and what looked like an entire bag of flour came pouring down, landing with perfect aim on the top of Elijah's head.

There was a whoop from above, where Noel and Aquila were dancing on the landing in their nightshirts.

"Heavens!" It was Wallace. He was standing in the doorway of the drawing room, mouth hanging open like a character in a comic book. Elijah stood frozen, his arms and face covered in flour. Despite the awful timing, Alex had to admit he did look very funny. Then the vicar turned and glared at the children.

"I think I may assure you," he hissed. "That I will *never* send a child of mine to live in a Bedlam like this!"

And he stalked up off the stairs, like a furious crow.

"Oh dear," sighed Marian, after the younger

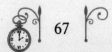

children had been scolded and threatened with various unlikely punishments. "We don't seem to be doing very well with Elijah, do we? But what was all that talk about Edith coming here?"

"That was us," said Ruby. "We told him he shouldn't send her to Scotsborough. It's – *very important*." She gave Marian a meaningful glance.

"Great Caesar!" It was the children's father. "You don't mean to say that confounded brother of mine is sending that little scrap to *Scotsborough*? I wouldn't send a dog there, let alone a child."

"Why, whatever's wrong with it?" said Wallace.

His father looked serious. "I have attended at Scotsborough many more times than I would like," he said. "Those little ones are more likely to graduate by the grave than the front door."

"Oh! Like the school in *Jane Eyre*?" said Anne, interestedly.

Alex had no idea what she was talking about, but Ruby said, "Yes! Just like that!"

"Oh!" said Noel, and he clapped his hands over his mouth.

"But why would Uncle Elijah want to send his daughter somewhere so awful?" said Harold. "I mean, I know he's an ass, but he isn't *evil*."

"Well –" said Marian. "I didn't like to mention it before, but – Elijah made some unfortunate business investments last year, which have cost him dearly. He may have had very little choice in where to place his daughter."

She sighed.

"I confess I have been uneasy about Scotsborough, too. I wish Elijah would let her stay with us.

"What!" said Aquila, completely unabashed by her scolding. "Send Edith here! I like that! You tell *him* that *we* would not countenance—"

"*Aquila*," said Harold in a warning voice.

"Well, we would not!"

"*You* might not, because *you* are a little goose, but I'll be hanged if the rest of us Pilgrims send a cousin of ours to a place like that. The shame of it! Father, what can we do? We *must* be able to convince him otherwise, must we not?"

"Uncle Elijah?" Wallace made a noise that

sounded like *pfff*. "I wager it would not be easy."

"Oh, pish!" Charles waved his hand. "Elijah was not always such a miserable old goat. Why! As a boy he knew how to be jolly! We must remind him, that's all. Show him that there is nothing unChristian about making merry, and that a little chaos is no bad thing for a child."

"Great Scott!" cried Harold. "Like *A Christmas Carol*! We must give him the happiest Christmas he's ever had, and then he'll see what an ass he's been."

"You mean," Aquila's face was a picture of disgust. "We have to be *nice* to him?"

"Oh, the horror!" said her mother.

They sat for some time discussing strategy. Edith was due to go to school on Boxing Day, which left them very little time. It was agreed that the children would concentrate on giving Edith the best Christmas possible – "So he can see how happy she'd be living here" – while the adults concentrated their efforts on Elijah himself. The Pilgrims were full of ideas about what might make their relations happy:

"Let's go ice skating!"

"And play charades – why, Elijah used to love charades as a child!"

"And we must go to Midnight Mass – t'will show him we are not such an unChristian family as all that."

It all sounded rather implausible to Alex, and the time scale alarmingly short. But the eager support of the others was comforting, and he allowed their enthusiasm to persuade him.

At last, Marian looked at the clock and gave a start.

"Mercy!" she cried. "It's half past the hour! Bed, for all of you! Quick!"

Going to bed was another challenge. There was no bathroom, nor, as far as Alex could tell, any running water at all, except for the pump in the yard. The toilets were in two small outbuildings at the back of the house. It was very dark and icy cold – you had to take a lantern out with you and

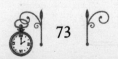

balance it on the floor while you did your business. Inside the building, there was a wooden seat with a hole in it and a wooden lid and underneath it a … well, a *pit* where the wee and the poo went. There was no toilet paper. Instead, there were neat squares of newspaper hanging from a nail on the back of the door. There was also a metal bucket filled with earth and ash, and a small shovel. After you'd been to the toilet, you had to tip a shovelful on to the waste below to dampen the smell. It wasn't entirely successful.

There was no sink. After he'd finished, Alex took the lantern and, rather self-consciously and much to the amusement of Wallace and Harold, washed his hands at the pump. He wasn't about to get cholera if he could help it.

The pump water was so cold it was like washing his hands in ice.

Alex was to sleep on a trundle-bed in Harold and Wallace's room, while Ruby was to share with Anne.

Marian handed them their nightclothes, saying, "I dare say it will all be a little queer, and not what you are used to, but I hope you shall be happy – they're good children, you know, and they mean well, though they are a little exuberant at times." She smiled at Ruby. "Alice will be along to unlace you and brush your hair."

"I hope Alice hurries up," Ruby said, as Marian

disappeared down the corridor. "This corset *itches*. What are your pyjamas like? I bet I've got – yep, look. Ankle-length white Victorian nightdress. And a – urk, a frilly bonnet thing!"

But Alex didn't have pyjamas. When Ruby saw what he *did* have, she fell about laughing.

"A nightshirt! And a nightcap! And bed socks! You're going to look like Wee Willie Winkie!"

"At least I don't need someone to *untie* me," said Alex.

Harold and Wallace's bedroom was big and cold. The carpet was thin and threadbare and didn't go all the way to the walls – Alex had never appreciated how amazing fitted carpets were before now. There was a jug full of hot water and a basin on a stand, which they were expected to use to wash and clean their teeth – there was a proper toothbrush with a bone handle, and toothpowder instead of toothpaste.

"Do we have to have the window open all night?" Alex asked. Even under a sheet, several blankets and a thick goose-feather eiderdown, he was still cold.

"Beastly, isn't it?" Harold agreed. "Do not worry, though – you'll warm up soon enough."

They lay in companionable silence, the little dog Bunyan curled up on the end of Wallace's bed.

"It should be a ripping Christmas anyway," said Wallace. "Ice skating tomorrow … and chopping

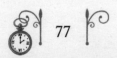

the Christmas tree down. And there'll be games…
I'll say this for the Pilgrims, we do know how to
have a jolly time."

"It sounds brilliant," said Alex. And despite
the cold and the open window and the Wee Willie
Winkie nightshirt, he meant it.

CHAPTER FIVE
CHRISTMAS EVE
MORNING

The morning was awful.

Some sort of magic had happened to Alex's bed overnight. It was blissfully warm, a sort of personal blanket sauna – the warmest Alex had been since landing in 1872. But the rest of the

room was so cold he could barely believe it was inside. It was so cold that there was ice – actual *ice* – on the inside of the open window, making strange, beautiful, fern-like patterns on the glass.

To get out of a your nice warm bed into a room that cold, to step on to a cold, worn bedside mat, to take off your lovely warm nightshirt and put on cold clothes that had sat on the chair all night... Alex knew they would warm up eventually, knew it would be easier once he was dressed and moving, but even so!

Well. It really made you appreciate central heating, that was all.

Alex had somehow always imagined the Victorians as rather prim and proper. Rich children, he'd thought, had all lived tucked away in nurseries at the top of the house, looked after by nannies. Perhaps that was true in some houses, but not here. Here, morning was a noisy, chaotic clamour, full of cries:

"Look here! Where's my clean collar? You've taken it haven't you, Harold, you beast?"

"Wallace! Stop using all the hot water! The rest of us have to wash too, you know!"

A new jug had been brought in by the maid, and they were expected to do a thorough head-to-toe wash with basin, jug and soapy flannel.

Noel and Aquila *did* have a nursery (two, in fact, a night nursery to sleep in and a day nursery full of toys). But they weren't tucked away at the top

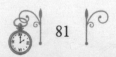

of the house, they were at the end of the corridor where Wallace and Harold and Anne slept, and the little children ran up and down the corridor in their nightclothes, giggling and shouting and sticking their faces in their brothers' and sisters' bedrooms, while Nanny ran after them and corralled one or the other back into the nursery. It made Alex feel rather dizzy, like he'd been bowled over by a pack of small Labrador puppies. He felt rather sorry for Edith, who looked terrified.

At last everyone was ready, and they all clattered downstairs for breakfast. First, however, was something called Morning Prayers. The whole household, including the children, Nanny, two housemaids, a manservant and Cook, all lined up in the hall while Elijah read a short Bible reading and a prayer. Everyone stood very solemnly while he did this, though Wallace and Ruby kept catching each other's eyes and trying not to giggle.

And then it was over.

"Grub!" cried Wallace. "Huzzah! I'm so hungry I could eat a horse!"

Alex had been wondering what Victorians ate for breakfast. Porridge? Bacon and eggs? Apparently not.

"Curry!" said Ruby, astonished. "Curry for breakfast!"

It was all laid out in little metal dishes on the table. As well as curry, there was something called

kedgeree, which was spicy rice with hard-boiled eggs and fish in it and kippers, which were an oily, smoky sort of fish. There wasn't a bowl of Cornflakes in sight. Alex thought the whole thing was hideous and made do with a plate of buttered toast.

Nobody noticed, though. Everyone was clamouring to be passed things, and poured tea, and complaining. "Latimer's taken all the kedgeree! It's too bad!"

Bunyan wriggled around under the table, getting in everyone's way and being fed surreptitiously with pieces of kipper. Uncle Elijah sat sipping his morning coffee and looking like a rather superior cat. Little Edith sat mute, watching them with round eyes.

"And what are your plans for the day, children?" said Marian, chewing on her toast with her elbows on the table and her hands all buttery, looking more like the eldest Pilgrim child than a mother of six. The children sat up at once.

"Christmas tree!" shouted Aquila, waving her fork in the air and spattering Uncle Elijah with curry. He wiped it away with a fastidious napkin and Aquila giggled. "Goodness, I am sorry. You'd like to come and chop down a Christmas tree, wouldn't you, Edith?"

"No, come with us!" cried Wallace, bouncing in his chair. "We're collecting holly and ivy and mistletoe, and we always have a capital time. We

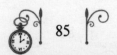

must have something to decorate the house at Christmas, you know."

"I rather thought we might go skating," said Harold. "Have you ever been skating, Uncle Elijah? I can't think of a jollier way to spend Christmas Eve, can you?"

Uncle Elijah's face was a picture of horror. Anne gave a splutter of laughter. Alex couldn't blame her. The thought of Uncle Elijah slithering about on the ice *was* pretty funny.

If Marian shared her amusement, she didn't show it.

"No, indeed!" she said. "You can all go to the lake together, and Harris can take the cart down for the tree. Elijah must be eager to spend these last few days with his little girl – must you not, Elijah? – and as entertainment this will do very well. A capital plan!"

Elijah opened his mouth. Then he caught Edith's eye, and shut it again.

After breakfast, the cart and the dog-cart (whatever that was) was ordered, and everyone rushed around hunting for cloaks, hats, gloves, muffs, ice skates and boots. Alex had a coat and a rabbit-skin hat; Ruby a cloak and a snood and a fur muff.

The dog-cart turned out to be a little one-seat carriage, ordered for Marian who was going into town to do some last-minute shopping. Alex had

thought Victorian women were driven about by coachmen, but Marian seemed quite happy to drive herself, and set off with a cheerful wave of her whip to a chorus of "Goodbyes!" from the children.

The Pilgrims also owned an old farm-cart, which was pulled by a beautiful brown horse – Edith's eyes went even rounder when she saw him and was permitted to stroke his nose and feed him an apple. It was driven by the manservant, whose name was Harris. The picnic hamper and the tools were to ride in this, and the rest of them were to walk. The lake wasn't far. In Alex's day it was a nature reserve and picnic spot. They often used to go there and feed the ducks when they were small.

They set off as a crowd, down what in modern times was a tarmacked road and here was a muddy, potholed track, bordered by wild-looking hedgerows full of wintry vegetation. The three grown-ups, Father, Elijah and Nanny, walked at the back, while the children ran on ahead, with Bunyan barking and yapping at their feet.

"Oh, isn't Christmas the jolliest time of year!" Aquila skipped joyfully backwards, her skirts already spattered with thick, claggy mud.

"I suppose so." Ruby looked thoughtful. "I mean, I do like Christmas, obviously. But our Christmases aren't much like this."

"Why! Is Christmas so different in America? How so?"

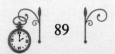

"Oh –" Ruby hesitated. "Well, it's smaller – there's only Alex and me and – er – our mum. I mean, we have presents and so forth, but there isn't all this" – she waved her hand vaguely – "noise."

"What are your Christmases like?" Alex asked Edith, who was stumping along beside them in a

little black coat and cap. She jumped.

"Oh!" she said. "We go to church in the morning. And the regiment have a party for the children. I got an orange last year."

"That sounds nice," said Alex doubtfully.

"But you have presents and things, don't you?"

said Aquila. "And holly and ivy and Christmas pudding, and crackers?"

"Not in India, you goose!" said Wallace.

"I have presents, of course," Edith said. "At least ... I did when Mamma was alive. I suppose Father will give me something this year. Last year he gave me a Prayer Book," she finished rather uncertainly.

"Mother will give you something better than a Prayer Book," said Wallace.

"And we all bought you... Oh!" Little Noel clasped his hand over his mouth. "That was supposed to be a surprise!"

"Noel, you goat!" cried Wallace, as Edith exclaimed, "Oh, was I supposed to buy you presents? I haven't bought a thing, and now it's too late, for it's Christmas tomorrow, and I only have ninepence, and there are so many of you!"

"Of course you do not, cousin," said Harold. "Goodness, it is bad enough for *us* and they're our own foul brothers and sisters. And it's only going to get worse," he added darkly. "Latimer *will* insist on breeding, and then I suppose Anne will start. Why! Just think if we all had six children each, that would be … would be…"

"Thirty-six nieces and nephews," said Ruby helpfully. "No, six of them would be your own children, I suppose."

"Even worse," said Anne. "For you couldn't get away with giving your own children boxes of

comfits, you know."

Edith was looking from one to the other in bewilderment. She didn't seem at all sure whether they were teasing her or not. Harold noticed, and gave her an affectionate bump with his shoulder.

"Do not worry, cousin!" he said. "I'll wager you'll soon be used to us."

⁂

Alex had supposed that the countryside would look much the same in 1872 as it did in modern times, but the further they walked, the more differences he noticed. The biggest change, of course, was the lack of tarmac roads and paths; Victorian country roads were little more than dirt tracks. Without cars, the countryside was weirdly quiet, although the birds more than made up for it. Even in winter, there seemed to be birds everywhere. A whole rookery of rooks at the end of the road. The hedgerows were full of the dart and song of little brown bodies.

And there were more insects. There were little beetles in the grass, and hibernating snails in a row on the beams in the toilet, and spiders webs all stiff with frost. (There were black beetles in Applecott House too, and scamperings in the night which Wallace said were mice.) Everything looked – well – *wilder*. The hedgerows were thick and messy with different grasses and plants – Alex didn't know the name of most of them. The trees were old and horny-looking, and even the

95

fields looked more unkempt. And it was much colder than modern Christmases. The ground was hard with frost, and their breath came out in grey clouds. It looked like a picture-book idea of winter.

Harold and Anne were to lead the skating-party. Ruby had been given Harold's skates, which attached to the bottom of your boots. She and Alex had both been skating at the local ice rink, but neither had ever skated on a real, live frozen lake like this.

Edith, after some hesitation, was to join them in Noel's skates. She seemed to have taken rather a fancy to Anne, who had declared her "A duck!" and had promised to teach her to skate.

"On the lake?" said Elijah, with a dark look at the frozen lake. Edith had a thick coat, but Elijah had nothing, just his usual black outfit. Alex remembered what Marian had said about him not having much money. Did he really not own a *coat*? He supposed he wouldn't need one in India, but *still*! His face was even whiter than usual, and the tips of his fingers were turning blue. "Is that really safe?"

"Oh, perfectly!" said the children's father cheerfully. "It has been frozen solid for weeks now. Will you not take a turn on the ice? I remember you were rather good as a child."

"I think not!" Elijah looked horrified.

His brother grinned.

"Look here, old chap, you'd better have a try. You'll freeze to death if you don't warm yourself up somehow. You should have taken my old overcoat when I offered it, but if you would not, you must do a little exercise, and what better than skating?"

"I – I mean. I don't—"

"Oh, pish!" Anne put her arm in his. "*Do* come, Uncle Elijah, it's ever so jolly."

And still protesting, they led Elijah towards the edge of the lake.

Wallace waggled his eyebrow at Alex.

"I say!" he said. Alex smiled back, but inside, he didn't feel so hopeful. Two days to turn this man around! Was it possible?

Noel and Nanny and Wallace were to form the

greenery-gathering party. There was a surprising amount of holly and ivy and pine trees and so forth around the lake; Alex had never really noticed them before, but once he did, he couldn't help seeing them everywhere. He wondered if it was the same in modern Britain. Woods didn't change *that* much, did they?

That left Harris and Father and Aquila, who were going to cut down the Christmas tree.

"Just go into a wood and cut it down?" said Alex. "Is that *allowed*?"

"No, indeed!" said Father. "But these woods all belong to Oakden – the big house in the village, you know. And the owners are old friends of ours, so each year they give us a tree."

"It is the most capital fun!" said Aquila. "We take our axes and we chop – and we chop – and we chop –"

"Coming?" said Father, and Alex decided that he was.

CHAPTER SIX
THE HOLLY, THE IVY
AND THE FIR

It was a strange feeling, looking for your Christmas tree in an actual wood. They crunched through the frost, Harris carrying the axe, Father a bag full of thick cord. Above their heads, the wood was alive with the flutter and rustle of tree-branches and

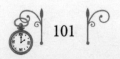

birds. Alex could feel the excitement bubbling in his stomach. A Victorian Christmas!

Both Father and Aquila took choosing the tree *very* seriously. Several were rejected as too lopsided, or too ugly. Several as too small. One was very nearly chosen, until Father noticed a branch which had been torn away, leaving an ugly mark on the trunk.

"It has to be *just right*," said Aquila.

At last, one was agreed upon and the chopping began. It took much less time than Alex had imagined, though he supposed this wasn't exactly surprising when you thought about it. It wasn't as though pine trees had thick trunks after all.

Carrying it back to the cart was harder. At the

garden centre where Alex's parents bought their tree, they did it up in a sort of plastic net to make it easier to carry. The children's father did his best with the cords, but the effect was rather clumsy. Everyone grabbed a bit of branch and made the best of it. It wasn't very heavy, but it *was* bulky and uncomfortable, and the pine-needles pricked against your hands. At last, however, they were back at the lake, where they were greeted with enthusiastic whoops from the others, who rushed to help load it into the cart.

"How's it going?" Alex whispered to Ruby.

Ruby grinned. "Look!"

She gestured out on to the lake. Harold was holding on to Elijah's hand and pulling him over

the ice. Clearly unstable, he wobbled about like a little black-limbed marionette, arms outstretched.

"Oh dear."

There was a dry little noise behind him. Alex turned. It was Edith.

She was laughing.

Ruby raised her eyebrows at Alex. Then she began to laugh, too.

After the tree was safely stowed in the cart, the tree-choppers fell to helping the greenery-gatherers. Alex was issued with a large pair of scissors and set to cutting bits of holly from a bush by the lake. Harold, to his astonishment, scrambled up one of the taller trees to bring down a bunch of mistletoe.

"That's mistletoe?" Alex said. He hadn't known

it grew on trees. But there it was, a sort of clump of it high up in the treetop, like a green and romantic crow's nest.

Around noon, just as they were beginning to get hungry, Nanny announced that it was time for lunch. The skaters were called in from the lake, and provisions unpacked from the coach. There were jacket potatoes wrapped in layers of cloth, each ready salted, with a pat of melted butter in their centre. With them, were Thermos flasks of hot tea. (Thermos flasks! How could the Victorians have no indoor toilets and *Thermos flasks*?) This was followed by something called jumble, which was a sort of gingerbread.

"What was the skating like?" Alex said to Ruby.

"Amazing. And Edith was brilliant – weren't you, Edith? She went at about a hundred miles an hour – once she worked out how to do it."

"Only because Anne was pulling her," muttered Aquila. Wallace elbowed her in the ribs.

Alex glanced at little Edith, chewing away at a piece of jumble. Her cheeks were flushed with the exercise, and she looked somehow more … *alive* than he'd ever seen her before.

"Did you like it?" he said.

"Oh, *yes*!" And then, as though rather embarrassed by her enthusiasm, she added, with a burst of confidence, "We don't have *anything* like that in India."

Uncle Elijah had taken his jacket potato and was eating it alone on the edge of the frozen lake. He looked like an awkward, ungainly sort of bird, perched on the tree-stump with his long black arms and legs splayed below him. Alex kept looking at him and thinking how cold he must be. He picked up one of the Thermos flasks and went over.

"Excuse me," he said. "I wondered – I brought you some tea. I thought you might be cold."

Elijah was reading a small, leather-bound book that was full of what looked like prayers. He inclined his head.

"I am perfectly comfortable," he said stiffly. "But I am grateful for your consideration."

He seemed to expect Alex to pour the tea, so Alex did so and handed him the cup. Elijah held it in his long hands, which were covered in red sores, like blisters. The other Pilgrims had them too. Chilblains, they were called. Alex had had no idea the past was so cold.

"Christmas can get a bit much, can't it?" Alex said, sympathetically. "It's bad enough at home and there are only four of us."

"A bit – ah, yes! What a quaint phrase. I own, there are rather too many children in this house for my tastes."

"Mine too," said Alex sympathetically. He liked the Victorian Pilgrims, but he was glad he didn't live in this Applecott House. There were people

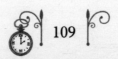

everywhere. He wondered how anyone ever got any time on their own. Presumably it was easier in summer when you could go and hide in the garden, and when the spare bedrooms didn't have people in them. But even so.

There was an awkward pause. There was something Alex had been wanting to say to Elijah, but he didn't quite know how to bring it up. It wasn't at all the sort of thing a child could say to a grown-up. But their deadline was in two days. Elijah was taking Edith to Scotsborough on Boxing Day. And if he did – well, who knows what would happen? Alex was getting rather fond of little Edith. Even if she didn't actually *die*, she would definitely have a horrible time.

And if he and Ruby didn't solve the problem they'd been sent to solve, they might never go home.

He took a deep breath. Just thinking about saying such a grown-up thing to a grown-up person made him feel weird. And Elijah wasn't at all the sort of person who invited confidences. And yet, somehow, that made it a bit easier. Elijah was an outsider, like Edith was. Perhaps he needed a friend too?

"I just..." He hesitated. Elijah looked up enquiringly. "I expect everyone is going to be making you do a lot of singing carols and so forth. And ... well, I don't think they always remember that your wife died. And probably you're quite

sad about that. I mean, I would be. So. I'm sorry. If they're too full on. They want you and Edith to be happy here. That's all."

Elijah stared at him.

"Good heavens," he said.

"From what Edith said, your wife sounded nice," he said. "So I bet you must miss her a lot."

There was another pause. "You are quite right," Elijah said. "I loved her very much indeed."

Alex nodded.

"The Pilgrims are nice really," he said. "Honestly they are. They're just a little over-enthusiastic."

Elijah grunted. He picked up his book and looked at it pointedly. Alex took the hint.

Back at the house it was, as Harold had threatened, all hands to work. The Christmas tree had to be dragged into the drawing room and secured in a pot (though the decorating itself was a great secret and was to be done by Marian and Father). Everyone else was set to decorating the house with armloads of greenery. It was a serious business, Alex discovered, but surprisingly good fun.

Halfway through the afternoon more guests arrived: Marian's mother, a cheerful-looking old lady in a white bonnet with a mysterious collection of parcels and carpet-bags and baskets, and Latimer, the children's oldest brother, with his laughing wife Louise, their baby son Teddy, and Teddy's Nana. The new arrivals were greeted

with great enthusiasm and excitement (and much yapping from Bunyan), Teddy was exclaimed over and cuddled, and the decorations admired.

"My! Haven't you grown?" Grandmamma exclaimed at each new child, which made Alex laugh, because it was just what his grandmother always said. "And where is little Edith?"

Edith flushed. She looked at Grandmamma with a curious mixture of fear and hopefulness. Grandmamma knelt down beside her and said, "I knew your father when he was smaller than you are now. Your grandmother was a dear friend of mine, and I have thought of you so often, growing up in that strange land. I hope we shall be great friends, you and I."

Edith went, if possible, even pinker. But she seemed pleased. Did Elijah like Marian's mother? If so, he gave no sign of it besides a stiff bow in her direction. And then there were more exclamations and excitement, until Marian cried, "Good heavens! Is that the time? Quick, everyone, or we'll never be dressed in time for dinner!"

A general rush upstairs. Marian followed them on to the children's corridor and shut the door behind her.

"Well!" she said. "And how goes our endeavour? What luck?"

The children all started talking at once, telling her about Elijah on the ice.

"I don't think he *liked* it exactly, but it was frightfully funny –"

"Her father bought her a prayer book for Christmas!"

"And Edith was *laughing*!"

"A *prayer book*!"

"Why is he like that?" Wallace demanded. "He couldn't be more different to Father! Was he found on the doorstep?"

"Oh…" Marion sighed. "He had a hard time as a child – I knew both brothers, as children, you know?"

"You've only told us about a thousand times," said Harold.

"Well. Elijah is very much the younger brother.

When Charles was fifteen and Elijah seven, their father died, and their mother was forced to remarry – she had no other way to support herself, you understand."

Ruby scowled. Alex could feel "Couldn't she get a job?" coming, and he said hurriedly, "And they got a wicked stepfather?"

"Quite so. Charles was at school, and then at the university, but poor Elijah and his mother had a terrible time of it. He was sent away and barely allowed to see his brother, and when he was home he was treated as an inconvenience. It broke his mother's heart – and Charles' too, of course. His stepfather died when Elijah was eighteen, but by then his relations with the family were damaged

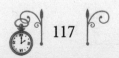

forever. I do not believe he has ever forgiven Charles, though I assure you there was little Charles could do about it. He was a child himself."

"Blimey," said Ruby.

"Indeed," said Marian. "I had hoped this visit might facilitate a reconciliation, but…"

"It will," said Alex. "It must!"

"It better had," Ruby muttered. "Or we'll be stuck here forever."

Christmas Eve dinner was evidently an important affair in the Victorian house, just as it was going to be for Aunt Joanna's bed-and-breakfast guests. There were real candelabras, and three courses, and what were evidently the nice dinner plates.

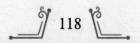

Afterwards there was coffee, which the grown-ups sat around sipping and gossiping over, just like they did at family parties at Aunt Joanna's house. The children, who had all finished dinner before the adults did, were desperate for the games to start.

"Oh, *do* hurry!" Aquila moaned. "How can people possibly take such *hours* to sit around *talking*?"

They abandoned the dinner party in disgust and went off to play in the hallway, until at last Marian and Grandmamma and Anne and Louise came out.

"*More* waiting," Aquila howled. "Now it's port and cigars and all that rot. I do think it's unfair.

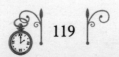

When I have my own house, I shall make the men leave and all us *women* will drink champagne. And serve them right!"

"Hear, hear!" said Ruby.

Marian laughed. "Come on," she said. "Let's go and see the drawing room. The poor old men will have to wait for *that*."

The drawing room door had been locked all through dinner. Marian disappeared inside to prepare.

"Come," she said, and the door opened and they all filed solemnly in.

The room was dark. The gas had been dimmed, and in the corner was the Christmas tree, hung with baubles and angels. Most were unfamiliar, but – yes! – there were the little drummer boys and the little angel that still hung on Aunt Joanna's tree. How brilliant! And best of all, the tree was lit with dozens of little candles, all pinned to the branches, all with little yellow flames amongst the greenery. There were paper chains hung from the ceiling, and a great quantity of holly piled on the mantelpiece. An enormous bunch of mistletoe hung from the chandelier in the centre of the room, and every candle on the chandelier was lit. There was an enormous fire crackling in the grate, and after the dull, cold dimness of the gaslit world, it was a dazzling sight. For once, all the children were silent. Then...

"Oh!" It was Edith.

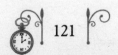

Her face was flushed, and her thin hands were clasped at her breast. Alex, looking at her, was astonished. She looked like a different child – she looked, in fact, for the first time as though she might actually be a Pilgrim.

"Oh!" she said. "Oh, it's lovely!"

There was a surprised silence.

Then from behind Alex another voice said,

"Indeed it is. Very lovely indeed."

It was Uncle Elijah. There was a look in his eye which Alex had never seen before. They all gawped at him. Then the other children started noisily telling Marian how beautiful it all was, and how clever she was, and what a capital tree it was, and the moment passed.

CHAPTER SEVEN
CHARADES AND CAROLS

The grown-ups moved into the drawing room, and sat by the fire, talking politely. Aquila hopped up and down in the doorway.

"My boots!" she said. "I think it might be working! Did you see? For a moment there he

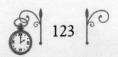

almost looked happy!"

"It has to work!" said little Noel. He looked uncharacteristically fierce. "We can't let him send Edith off to die!"

"Oh Lord!" said Harold, scowling at his brother.

"Noel! You little goose!" said Anne.

Edith stammered, "What do you mean? I'm not –?"

Alex and Ruby exchanged glances.

"It's nothing –" said Alex quickly.

But Ruby had already started talking. "It's your school," she said. "Scotsborough. It's – well, it's not a very nice place. We don't *know* that you'd die, but –"

"But – if Father wishes me to go there, it cannot

– he would not –"

"Has your father actually *been* there?" said Ruby.

"Oh no! But the Reverend Hill recommended it most highly. He said it was a most Christian place, and it would be well for Father to support such a worthy institution."

"Well! I like that!" said Harold. "And has the Reverend *Hill* been there? Our father has and he says it's a rotten place."

Edith looked confused. "I don't – the Reverend Hill is a most devout man – he wouldn't –"

"What the deuce has devout got to do with it?" said Wallace. "He lives in India! Why should your father trust his opinion above our own *father*'s?"

Edith went pink.

Anne said, "Oh, come! Uncle Elijah does not like Mother and Father, you know he does not. There's no shame in that, Edith. Mother and Father do not like him much, either. He is only here because he would consider it unseemly not to visit his brother at Christmastime."

"I wouldn't listen to someone I didn't like over a friend of mine," said Alex, trying to be fair. "And neither would you, I bet. If *Uncle Elijah* told you the school you were going to send your daughter to was wrong and you ought to let her live with him instead, you wouldn't listen to him, *would* you?"

There was a pause, while everyone thought

about Uncle Elijah.

"Indeed, no!" said Aquila.

"But *Father*," said Wallace. "You couldn't compare –"

"My father does not like your mother, it's true," said Edith in a low voice. "But –"

There was no time for more. They could hear voices and footsteps in the hallway. The men were finished with their brandy, and the games were about to begin.

The children – except for Edith, who still looked a little wide-eyed – cheered up immediately at the prospect of games.

Elijah looked horrified.

127

"I think I may retire early," he murmured. "A man of the cloth – parlour games – it would not—"

"Oh, pish!" said Charles, taking his arm. "What, come back from India for so short a time and spend it hiding in your room! Nonsense! Why, when you were a little thing, you loved to play at charades!"

Elijah stiffened.

"I must have been a very little thing indeed, for I do not remember it."

The temperature in the room seemed to have dropped by several notches. They were saved by Grandmamma, who said gently, "Do stay, Elijah dear. We have so little time with you, and we have missed you so much. I know the little girl would be sorry if you went."

Everyone looked at Edith, who stared back at them with her rabbit-in-headlights expression. Elijah looked for a moment as though he were going to argue, then he sat himself down with a sullen look.

"As you wish," he said.

Wallace waggled his eyebrows at Alex.

"Imagine Uncle Elijah playing parlour games!" he said.

They started with Twenty Questions. Someone picked an object and said whether it was an animal, a vegetable or a mineral. (Animal included people, vegetable anything plant-based, and mineral everything else – so Queen Victoria counted as

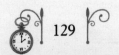

an animal, Marian's cotton handkerchief counted as vegetable, and Applecott House was mineral.) Then everyone else got twenty questions to guess what the object was (the person who knew the answer was only allowed to answer "yes" or "no").

Edith sat by her father and said very little. Elijah sat through the first couple of rounds with a superior expression, until suddenly he said, "Roderick Random!"

Harold, whose turn it was to answer questions, looked very surprised and said, "Yes! Golly! However did you know that?"

But the suspicion of a smile twitched the corner of Elijah's mouth. "It was hardly a taxing problem," he said stiffly.

Harold gawped. "Fancy you liking Roderick Random!" he said.

Uncle Elijah's smile disappeared immediately. "As to that," he said, "the follies of my youth are far behind me."

And he refused to be drawn into the rest of the game.

After Twenty Questions, Marian announced that they were going to play Charades. Alex was a bit surprised about this; he knew how to play charades, and it didn't sound very Victorian. In the version he knew, you had to pick a film or a TV show or a book and then get everyone else to guess it by breaking it down into words or syllables and acting them out.

Victorian Charades was quite different. It was played in teams. Each team picked a word which could be broken down into syllables which were also words – the first team did Handkerchief, which broke down into hand – cur (a dog, apparently) – and chief. They then had to put on four little plays, one for "hand", (they did a very funny play in which Harold asked Ruby for her hand in marriage and her papa refused to give them permission because Harold was only a poor chimney sweep), one for "cur" (Bunyan, of course, played the dog), and one for "chief" (they did a historical play for this one – the death of Captain Cook in Hawaii). Then the final play was "handkerchief": a pitched battle between the Yorkists and the Lancastrians, whoever they were, which ended with the children's father surrendering, and begging for mercy on his knees, a white handkerchief tied to a stick as a flag of surrender.

All the Pilgrim children took this game very seriously and seemed to possess a surprising number of shawls and hats and wooden swords and other props. They spent ages arguing about the plays, and what should happen in them, and who should be what.

Uncle Elijah absolutely refused to take part in Charades. The children begged and their father said, "Oh come, Elijah! 'Twas your favourite game when you were a child."

But Elijah was adamant.

"*You'll* play though, won't you, Edith?" Noel said, rather shyly. He took her hand. "We're going to have a princess in ours, and I want her to be you."

His brothers and sisters made loud vomiting noises.

"A princess! No fear!"

"What rot, Noel!"

"Noel, you are a scrub!"

But Noel was insistent.

"I am not. I think Edith would make a very good princess."

"Quite right," said Marian. "And so she shall! Come along, Edith."

And despite the others' groans, Edith appeared as the Princess Royal, in a scene where everyone was trying to tell her that a pipe had burst in the palace, but couldn't because whenever she turned to look at them they had to stop talking and bow. The idea was to show the "bow" part of rainbow, which they did to great applause.

"Bravo!" cried Marian. "Didn't she do well, Elijah dear?"

Elijah regarded his daughter in silence. Alex thought for a terrible moment that he wasn't going to say anything.

"But of course," he said.

Edith went pink.

After the games, Edith and Noel were bundled off to bed. Aquila, after much pleading, was allowed to stay up, and they set off for Midnight Mass.

It was very dark outside. Much darker than night-time in the twenty-first century. No street lights. No car headlights. No torches even – just lanterns on long poles, like something on a Christmas card. Aquila and Alex held one each; Alex felt very grand walking down the dirt path with it swinging over his head. They all had hats – and the girls had muffs – made of real rabbit fur, which were gloriously warm and soft.

The air outside was crisp and cold. The frosty grass made a delicious *crunch*ing sound when you stepped on it, and their breath came out in

clouds of frost. The children called excitedly to each other as they hurried down the lane while the adults walked along behind, just like they did in the twenty-first century.

The little church was full of people; everyone

from labourers in ragged overcoats to servants in crisp white aprons, to a smart-looking party who Alex guessed must come from Oakden House. The whole church was lit with gaslights, which gave it a strange, dim, rather eerie feeling. And there was a little black stove at the front, with bright orange flames which blazed away when the curate opened the door to shovel in more coal. There was greenery everywhere: holly on the altar, trails of ivy over the doorway, a Christmas tree by the doorway lit with tiny candles in amongst the branches. Even the familiar red painted devils' faces on the ends of the beams had been wrapped in ivy; they didn't seem to know quite what to make of this festivity but were bearing it with good humour. And

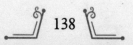

everywhere friends of the Pilgrims were waving and calling to them, and children were running about in the aisles, and Bunyan was yapping at a small boy who was teasing him with a red rubber ball.

Alex was used by now to seeing familiar things transformed by time, but the church was particularly odd, because it was so *old* to start with. It was medieval, and though he knew vaguely that some bits of it – like the pews and the footrests and the noticeboard with details of Zumba classes and Guide meetings – were of course newer, he'd somehow imagined that it had always looked vaguely like this for hundreds and hundreds of years.

It was strange therefore to see how different everything looked. The footrests were gone, and though the pews were still there, they looked much newer and shinier. The wooden boards at the end of the church with the lists of the war dead were gone too, of course, and all sorts of odd things like the lectern and the little table with the collection boxes on it had been moved around or replaced with other churchy sorts of things. There was a stack of pamphlets about missionaries in Africa, and – how funny! – a stack of very old-fashioned-looking copies of *The Church Times*, just like there were in modern Dalton.

Alex and Ruby's parents didn't go to church, but Alex had been to the Remembrance Day service a couple of times with the Scouts, so he knew what to expect. The Christmas service was something special, though. The people settled in their seats, the organ began to play, and here was the choir, walking up the aisle – Wallace and Harold among them, looking unexpectedly angelic – holding lighted candles and singing *O Come, All Ye Faithful.*

Then there were some dull bits – the call and responses from the vicar, the communion, a sermon about the Importance of Helping the Poor, then more singing: *Once in Royal David's City* and *Tomorrow Shall Be My Dancing Day.* It could almost have been the carol concert at Alex's school. And then it was midnight, and the church

bells were all ringing, and the vicar called, "Merry Christmas, my good people! Merry Christmas!"

And the choir were filing back up the aisle singing *Hark the Herald Angels Sing!* and Marian turned, smiling, to the children and said, "Merry Christmas, my dears!"

And Aquila was bouncing up and down on her seat, shouting, "It's Christmas! It's Christmas Day!"

CHAPTER EIGHT
CHRISTMAS MORNING

"I say! Wake up, you lazy beasts, wake up! It's Christmas!"

Alex rolled over and rubbed his eyes. Noel and Aquila were standing in the doorway, clutching their stockings, Edith hovering behind them

anxiously. Aquila was holding a lighted candle in a Wee-Willie-Winkie-ish holder.

"It's stocking time!" she said, waving her stocking in the air.

There was a groan from the general direction of Harold's bed.

"Didn't anyone ever teach you kids to respect your elders?" he said. "What time is it anyway?"

"I don't know, but it's ever so early," Aquila said, clambering on to his bed, while Noel shouted, "Early, early, early! The servants are up, but nobody else is. Can't you light the gas, then we can see what we've got?"

Another groan from Harold.

"I don't suppose we're going to get any sleep

now, are we? Go and bother the girls, why don't you, and we'll think about it while you're away."

He flopped back down on the bed. The room was dark – Alex had never realised quite what a bother it was, getting up before electric lights were invented. He sat up, and saw Wallace, also sitting up, fumbling with the candle and the box of matches on his bedside table. The match flared, the candle lit, and in its dim glow, Alex could see Wallace grinning at him.

"What ho!" he said. "You've got a stocking too!"

So he had. At home, Alex and Ruby hung out pillowcases for Father Christmas, which were filled with things like computer games and selection boxes and copies of *The Guinness Book of*

Records. Here, however, he had an actual woollen stocking, long and bulky and bulging in all sorts of interesting places.

"I'm going to light the gas," said Wallace. "Harold isn't going to move if he can help it – why,

I do believe the lazy beast has gone back to sleep! Wake up, Hal, you great lump! It's Christmas!"

He climbed out of bed and padded towards the gas sconce. He lit a match and the gas flared. There was a shriek from the doorway, and there were Anne and Ruby in their nightdresses.

"*Happy Christmas!*" Anne yelled, and launched herself at Harold with a war whoop.

"Happy Christmas," said Wallace, flopping down on Alex's bed, stocking in hand. "Sorry about the madhouse!"

"Are we waking Latimer?" said Anne, her long hair in a thick plait down her back. "Or is he too middle-aged for stockings now, do you think?"

"Practically geriatric," said Wallace. "Stockings

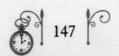

147

stop when you tie the knot – an excellent reason to stay single forever, say I. Oh, huzzah, look! *Twenty Thousand Leagues Under the Sea!* That's a capital book – have you read it?"

Alex hadn't. He had a book in his stocking. too: *The Coral Island*. And a candy-cane. And a wooden spinning top, and a sugar mouse in a paper bag, with a tail made out of string, and an apple and an orange, just like in stockings at home, and a pair of red woollen mittens, and a packet of home-made gingerbread, and a funny little wooden box with an engraved lid, and a tin trumpet. All the children had musical instruments, even Harold and Anne.

"For carols!" said Noel, whacking his drum.

Ruby's stocking was much more grown-up, which surprised Alex somewhat; he'd thought perhaps thirteen-year-olds were still children in Victorian times, but evidently not. She had a book too, *Little Women*, a set of embroidered handkerchiefs, a little bottle of perfume, and a set of pink notepaper and envelopes, as well as the mittens and the fruit and the sweets and the gingerbread and a penny whistle.

"These stockings are completely sexist!" she said, but Alex privately thought the contents were only old-fashioned versions of the sort of things she usually got. Last Christmas she'd had note cards and lipstick in black, green and purple, and she hadn't said anything about *them* being sexist.

And she already *owned* a copy of *Little Women*!

"You're just jealous because I didn't get handkerchiefs," he said. "What did you get, Edith?"

Edith was sitting on the bed surrounded by presents. The same gingerbread, the same sugar mouse, a little tin triangle, a rubber frog with a tongue which stuck out when you squeezed it. Good old Marian.

"I thought …" she said. "I wasn't sure … since Mother died…"

"What's your mother got to do with it?" said Noel. "Father Christmas brings stockings – everyone knows that!"

Edith blinked and Harold laughed.

"Of course he does," he said. He ruffled Edith's hair. "Mother's a good egg," he said. "Despite what your father thinks of her. She looks after the people who live in her house."

Edith looked from her stocking to Harold. Alex wondered what she thought of her noisy cousins. Did she *want* to live here? Would she back them up against her father if it came to a fight?

"Oh!" said Aquila suddenly. "Look – it's seven o'clock! That's practically afternoon! Let's wake Mother up and tell her so!"

"You didn't honestly think we could sleep through all this racket, did you?" Marian appeared in the doorway in her dressing-gown. "Merry Christmas, darlings! Goodness, what a mess!

You'd better get yourselves dressed and washed if you're going to be downstairs in time for prayers."

There was the now-familiar scramble for clothes and washstands, prayers in the hallway under the greenery, and a general charge into the dining room for breakfast. There was coffee for the adults and hot chocolate for the children, pancakes and crumpets and hot rolls and bowls of fruit.

"This is more like it!" said Ruby.

After breakfast there was bed-making again, then a rush to prepare the house for the day. Alex had assumed that if you had servants, you never had to do housework again, but this evidently wasn't true – he supposed that six children still living at home, plus all the Christmas visitors, must make a lot more mess than two maids could cope with. The servants were kept busy preparing the Christmas dinner, and the children were drafted in to sweep and mop the floors, tidy away the toys and the props from Charades, and generally make the house presentable.

Alex found himself in the dining room with Edith, polishing the table. For such a little person, Edith was a surprisingly good table-polisher, better than Aquila who had given up in disgust and gone to help with the Christmas baking. Edith worked in concentrated silence, then said suddenly, "Alex?"

"Hmm?"

"It is really so bad – my school, I mean?"

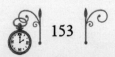

Alex didn't quite know how to answer this.

"Well –" he said. Then, "Yes. Honestly, it is. I know living here must be rather different to how you lived in India. But please, Edith, if you think you have *any* chance of persuading your father, please ask him to let you stay. At least you won't starve to death here."

Edith's eyes were fearful. Alex wondered if he'd done the right thing. But then there were more "Halloo!"s from the hallway, and more guests were here, and the others were calling for them to come and see.

There was Mr Thomas, the curate who gave the children lessons, the Reverend Phillips, straight from the Christmas Day service, and two old ladies who lived together in the village and seemed delighted with everything. They all squeezed into the dining room, and dinner began.

A Victorian Christmas dinner seemed to be rather similar to Christmas dinner at home, except that there were more people, and it was noisier, and there was suet pudding to start, and goose instead of turkey. There was still stuffing, though, and apple sauce, and lots of potatoes.

There was even pudding, although it was called "plum pudding" rather than "Christmas pudding". It tasted pretty much like ordinary Christmas pudding – a bit stickier, perhaps, and much bigger, and obviously homemade. And to Alex's disappointment, it didn't seem to have any

actual plums in it. It was set fire to and brought into the dining room by the children's father, with a big jug of cream.

"Big" presents came after dinner, just like they did in Alex and Ruby's house. Compared to the sort of presents Alex and Ruby usually got, the "big" presents were rather small (last Christmas Ruby had got a laptop and Alex a new bike). But with such a big family, there were a lot of them.

A surprising number of the presents seemed to be homemade. Aquila, who didn't strike Alex at all as a sewing-y sort of girl, had made pen-wipers with everyone's initials in the corner. They looked like little felt flowers, and were used for wiping pens. Alex wasn't sure why you'd need to wipe pens, but the wipers were rather nice. Anne had sewn wallets for everyone except the younger children, who each had two beautiful little felt mice in scarlet jackets, with little wire spectacles perched on their noses. Noel had made sweets, and Harold had drawn funny cartoons in little wooden frames.

The presents from parents weren't homemade, but they weren't anywhere near as big as a laptop. Anne got a bolt of green silk to make a dress out of. Wallace got roller-skates, which didn't sound at all Victorian to Alex. Baby Teddy got a wooden horse on wheels to ride on.

Alex and Ruby didn't have the great piles of presents that the other children did, but Marian

had made sure they weren't forgotten. Ruby got a workbox filled with all sorts of sewing things: needles, and thread, and pins, and a thimble, and a pincushion and a little pair of scissors. She looked horrified, but she managed to say "Thank you," far more politely than Alex had expected. He could see it was rather a nice present; he expected it had cost quite a lot of money.

Alex's own present was a pocket knife with a beautiful wooden holder and a single blade; like a sort of simple Swiss Army Knife. Both Noel and Aquila were rapturous in their admiration of this; apparently they were both considered too young for a knife of their own. Alex wasn't sure what he thought – it was a beautiful object, and children in old-fashioned books were always going on about owning their own knife, but he wasn't really sure what he was supposed to do with it. It wasn't like he spent hours in the woods cutting up firewood or whittling toys. It didn't even have a tin-opener attachment like Swiss Army Knives did (and even then, surely an actual tin-opener would be more useful?). Secretly, he thought Ruby's present was more interesting and practical. He would have liked to be able to make something as lovely as those little felt mice.

He did his best to sound pleased, though. He knew Marian had had to make a special trip to buy all their Christmas presents, and he *was* grateful.

Uncle Elijah's presents were just as awful as Edith had predicted. Edith got a leather-bound Bible. The Pilgrim children got books with titles like *Pious Tales for Small Hands*. Anne was given *Advice for Christian Maidens*. Her face when she opened it was such a picture of disgust that Alex wanted to laugh out loud. For a moment, she looked exactly like Ruby.

Marian, rather to Alex's surprise, gave Edith a knitted rabbit, with button eyes. Around its neck was a little leather purse, with half a crown inside it, which was apparently rather a lot of money.

"Perhaps you don't care for animals, dear," she said kindly to Edith, who was looking at the rabbit with a bewildered expression. "But I thought he might be a comfort when you're far from home and living with strangers."

Edith blinked, but said nothing. Alex saw her crook her arm protectively around the rabbit, and he thought that Marian might have had the right of it.

"A rabbit, though?" said Aquila, but Harold nudged her.

"Shhh. Father's giving Uncle Elijah his present."

"So?"

"So look!"

Uncle Elijah's present was an old-fashioned black-and-white family photograph. It showed a woman with a child between her knees, a man

with the most fabulous side-burns Alex had ever seen, and a teenage boy. They were standing very stiffly and formally in a photographer's studio, with a few ferns and so forth beside them.

Elijah's expression didn't change, but he stared at the photograph for a long time.

"It's you and I and Father and Mother," said Charles. "I thought – well, you're so far away in India. I thought you should have it. I didn't want you to forget your family."

Elijah cleared his throat.

"Yes, well," he said. "Well. Yes."

"Is that how Uncle Elijah looks when he's happy?" Wallace whispered to Edith. Edith blinked.

"He's either utterly disappointed or over the moon," said Ruby. "It's hard to tell."

CHAPTER NINE
A CHRISTMAS
CASTASTROPHE

After the present-opening was done, they settled into a sleepy, happy idleness, which felt very Christmassy indeed. The older children were deep in their new presents; Anne was poring over a pattern-book looking for the right dress to go with her bolt of silk while Harold was engrossed in *The Adventures of Peregrine Pickle*. Noel and Aquila were playing a noisy game of *Happy Families* on the floor, while the adults sat around drinking glasses of wine and smoking pipes and generally looking happy and lazy and full. Baby Teddy was asleep on his mother's lap, still wearing a paper sailor's hat from a cracker. Even Uncle Elijah looked almost happy, deep in a complicated Biblical argument with Mr Thomas the curate. They seemed to disagree about absolutely everything, and the more they disagreed, the more they seemed to enjoy themselves. Alex thought it was all just about perfect, except…

"Where's Edith?" he said.

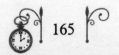

Ruby looked around.

"Gone to the loo?" she said doubtfully.

"She's been gone for ages if she has," said Alex. He stood up. Something was wrong; he could feel it, prickling down his back. "*Ruby*," he said, but Ruby seemed to feel it too.

"All right. I'm coming."

It was dark outside, and desperately cold. Edith wasn't in the outside toilet, and as far as they could tell in the light from the lantern, she wasn't anywhere in the yard. They didn't like to stay too long outside to check. The air cut like ice against Alex's cheeks. He shivered.

Edith was not in the day nursery. However, on her pillow in the night nursery was piece of paper.

Alex opened it warily. There was a message on it, written in unsteady pencil capitals.

I AM RUNING AWAY BECOS I
DO NOT WANT TO GO TO SCOOL.
I SHAL PROBLY BE A GIPSEE.

YOURS AFFECSHUNUTLY

EDITH PILGRIM

They looked at each other.

"She can't have gone far…" said Ruby doubtfully. "Not when it's so dark."

"And cold," said Alex, but little Edith out on

her own in the night was not something either of them liked to think about. "Come on," he said. "Let's tell the others."

They clattered downstairs and into the drawing room.

"Edith's run away!" Alex cried, waving the letter.

"Because of that awful school Uncle Elijah's sending her to!" said Ruby. "And I don't blame her!"

"She's going to be a gypsy!" said Aquila, reading the letter over Ruby's shoulder. "Great Caesar!"

"But she can't have gone out on her own in this weather!" said Marian. "What have you children been saying to her?"

"Nothing!" said Ruby indignantly. "I mean … well, we *did* tell her about Scotsborough, but only by mistake. We didn't think she'd be such a muppet as to go out on her own!"

"Her outdoor things are gone," said the children's father, from the doorway. "We'd better get a search party together."

A search party! They looked at each other, then at Elijah, whose face, if anything, was even whiter than before. Somehow, his narrow face and dull eyes no longer looked alarming, but just for a moment, he looked like a child.

"Children," their father was saying. "Do any of you have *any* idea where she might be going?"

They looked at each other.

"We have not been anywhere since she got here," said Harold doubtfully. "Just to the lake and to church…"

"I suppose she may be trying to get to Ipswich," said Marian. "But no, she couldn't! Not in the dark!"

"We must try the church," said the children's father. "It seems the most likely. And check the outbuildings. And ask in the village – perhaps someone has seen her. Oh, if only it was not Christmas! Everyone will be inside. Foolish child! What can she be thinking?"

"It's my fault," said Elijah suddenly. They all looked at him, amazed. His eyes were bleak. "I should have listened… I did not think…"

"Oh, hush," said Marian, suddenly on his side. "You could not have predicted this. Come! We shall find her! She cannot have gone far."

There was a great hurry of boots and coats and capes and hats and then – so quickly that Alex could hardly take it in – they were gone.

The younger children – Noel, Aquila, Wallace, Ruby and Alex – sat and looked at each other, rather aghast. Almost all of the adults had joined the search party. Only Grandmamma, the old ladies and the two nannies – Teddy's still clutching him to her chest – remained.

"I say," said Noel. He looked rather as though he was going to cry. "Is she going to get lost in the snow and die? Like the babes in the wood?"

 171

"There isn't any snow, goose," said Aquila grumpily. But you could see her heart wasn't really in it.

"I suppose she *has* left the house, hasn't she?" said Ruby. She had a visible air of pulling herself together. "I mean, nobody's actually looked, have they?"

"That's true enough." Harold brightened. "It would be pretty sickening if she turned out to be locked in a box room or something. Shall we check?"

The thought of having something to do cheered them all up. Teddy's nanny took him upstairs – he was beginning to fuss – and Grandmamma said she would wait in the drawing room in case Edith came home. But the others set off to explore the house.

It didn't take long. Edith wasn't in any of the bedrooms, or any of the public rooms. Nor was she in the kitchen.

"What about the servants' bedrooms?" said Alex.

Aquila looked shocked. "We cannot go in *there*!" she said.

"Why not?" said Alex. "Edith might have done."

"Do you honestly mean there's a whole bit of your house you've never been in?" said Ruby. "How *weird*." She and Alex knew every inch of Applecott House, of course; in their day, all the

servants' bedrooms were bed-and-breakfast rooms.

"They're private," said Aquila, and she wouldn't be budged. In the end, they compromised by asking Nanny to look for them.

But in any case, Edith wasn't there.

"Outhouses," said Harold. "Stables and so forth. Maybe she meant to run away and just ... could not manage it."

They put on their outdoor clothes and lit the lanterns. Searching by lantern-light! It ought to have been exciting, but there was a tight knot of fear in Alex's chest. The night was dark and icily cold, and the torchlight lit only a small circle of light around them. How easy it would be to miss something in the dark! How easy to walk past a small fallen figure all in black, a little heap of clothes in the darkness. If they didn't find Edith, she could die. Was *this* what they had been sent back to do? No, how could it have been, she wouldn't have run away if they hadn't been there. But still … they had been pulled out of their own time and dragged forcibly back into the past to right some wrong. Surely this search must be part of it? Alex wasn't sure of very much, but he was as sure as he could be that the adults' search party would be unsuccessful.

If anyone was going to find Edith, it would be them.

There were a lot of outhouses at Applecott House.

There was the outdoor toilet. The coach-house, which in the twenty-first century was where Aunt Joanna and her guests kept cars, but in 1872 was where the carriages lived. The gardener's sheds, full of plant pots and garden forks, and a garden roller, and a lawn mower that looked like it needed to be pulled by a horse.

And the stables.

Aunt Joanna's stables had long ago been sold and converted into houses. These stables were dark and warm and strangely alive. There was an office-type room with saddles and bridles and brushes and other bits of tack. And there were the horses' stalls. Their heads peered over the doors, eyes huge and liquid and knowing and curious.

Neither Alex nor Ruby particularly cared about horses, but these were undeniably beautiful. There were the two carriage horses, a horse which the children's father apparently rode to the hunt and to medical emergencies, and a fat pony which was shared between the children.

In the last stable, the pony was lying down on the straw. She lifted her head when she heard the children, but she did not move. Looking over the door, Alex could see why. Curled up in the straw beside her, fast asleep, still wearing her cloak and her hat and her fur muffler, was Edith.

It was much later. The searchers were back from the village, Edith had been hugged and kissed and scolded, and was sitting by the fire looking something between pleased and defiant. The grown-ups were drinking whisky and soda, and Wallace and Noel were roasting chestnuts in the fire shovel.

"But why did you *do* it?" Marian exclaimed.

Edith said, "I didn't want to go to school… I was going to run away and live with the gypsies, but it was so dark, I thought I'd better wait 'til morning."

"Live with the gypsies!" Marian looked at her, and then, quite suddenly, she laughed. "Goodness, child!" she said. "Carry on like this and you might be a Pilgrim after all."

Elijah sat by the fireplace, his face bent, his head in his hands. He looked bewildered, thought Alex, like a small child who's been ordered to do something that's just beyond his capabilities.

"She could have frozen to death..." he murmured. "She could have died..."

"Indeed no," said the children's father cheerfully. "Why, when I think of what my lot get up to! The time they decided to climb the ridge-pole of the stable roof ... the time they decided to play at bullfighting..."

"Charles!" said Marian, and he grinned. Fortunately, Elijah didn't seem to have taken in what he had said.

"Jenny was always so good at this..." he

murmured. "I never expected to have to…"

"You *don't* have to," said Marian. "Let Charles and I help you. We'd love to have Edith here, you know we would."

"I don't know," he said confusedly. "I just don't know."

Marian knelt beside him and took his hand.

"I know we aren't the family you would have chosen for Edith," she said. "We're a rough and ready lot, I own. But my children have good honest hearts and are happy and healthful. She'll come to no harm with us, I promise you that."

Elijah looked up and around the room. Alex looked round too, wondering what he was seeing. The happy, flushed faces of the children? The

chaos of Christmas toys and paper and dirty plates? Or Edith, her pinched little face with two red spots of colour as she watched her father, the anxiety in his eyes reflected back in hers?

"Why don't you ask Edith what *she* wants?" said Ruby suddenly. "It's her life, after all."

They all – except for Marian, who seemed rather amused – looked at her as though she were insane. Then Harold cried, "A capital idea! Why don't you?"

They all looked at Edith, who blushed, and hid her face in her shoulder.

Wallace said, "You *do* want to come to us, don't you, cousin? Say you do, and we'll have fine times!"

"You can be our pirate queen!" cried Noel. "And – and – the captured princess and all the things Aquila won't be!"

They turned to Aquila, who went red, and muttered, "If she wants to, I don't say it mightn't be useful. Now and then."

Marian smiled and held out her hand. "It must be your decision, my dear," she said. "But you know we'd love to have you."

Edith had gone even redder. Alex thought for a moment that she wasn't going to speak. Or perhaps she was going to say she wanted to go to a different school, or back to India with her father, or something awful like that? He realised suddenly that he had no idea what she thought of

her aunt and uncle and her cousins. Perhaps she had as low an opinion of them as her father did.

But at last she raised her head.

"I want to stay with Aunt and Uncle," she whispered. "And – and be a pirate queen like Noel said."

"Huzzah!" Noel cried.

And now every eye in the room was turned to Elijah. He seemed even more bewildered by the attention. He took his handkerchief out of his pocket and wiped his forehead with it, the decision seemingly too much for him. At last he said, rather jerkily: "I would – I would of course have to pay for her board, and – and she must be educated in the scripture, and—"

But what else Edith must be educated in was drowned out in cheers.

CHAPTER TEN
WHAT HAPPENED
TO EDITH

"Is that it, then?" said Ruby. "Can we go home now?"

"Let's go and see," said Alex.

They got up, unnoticed in the general excitement, and slipped into the hallway.

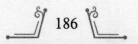

"All right!" said Ruby.

The mirror had opened. There was Aunt Joanna's hall, there was the tinsel wrapped around the bannisters, there was the edge of the Christmas tree, half decorated. You could almost hear the Christmas music playing from the kitchen radio.

"Let's go!" said Ruby. She grabbed his wrist. "Hey! Let's go dressed like this!"

"We can't!" said Alex, horrified. He'd seen how long Marian's darning had taken her last night. Sewing machines didn't seem to be a thing yet. How much painstaking work must it have taken Marian to make their outfits? Hours and hours and hours and hours. And how much money? That length of cloth had been Anne's entire

Christmas present. "Ruby, we can't, really. Not when they've been so kind to us. And nobody will believe us anyway. They never do. They'll just think we took them from the theatre cupboard at school or something."

Ruby wavered.

"This ought to be *provable*," she wailed. "It really ought! If only Marian hadn't been trying to come through the mirror! I had it all planned – I was going to bring my phone and *film* people. They wouldn't have been able to argue with that!"

"Hmm," said Alex. He rather sympathised with his parents, who had had to put up with months of Ruby insisting they take the mirror to MIT and get it tested. It just *sounded* so implausible.

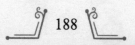

He wouldn't have believed them either.

"Come on," he said. "Let's get changed. We can take our Christmas stockings back anyway."

They ran upstairs and into the bedrooms. Nobody was there. Alex dressed quickly, leaving the Victorian clothes in a pile on the bed. He wished there was some way he could thank Marian, but the mirror was cagey about who it showed its secret self to. Someone could walk into the hallway at any minute, and it would put on its usual face again, and who knew how long they might be trapped here for?

The modern clothes felt strange and stiff and thin. He grabbed his Christmas stocking and his Christmas knife from the bedroom, and ran back

down the stairs.

Ruby appeared a moment later, looking very strange and out-of-place in her jeans and twentieth-century sweatshirt.

"Hurry up!" she said.

But the hall was still empty. Home still there in the mirror. Alex took a deep breath and stepped into the glass.

They landed on the floor in their usual heap. Here they were. Back in the twenty-first century once again. Alex looked around dazedly. How strange the familiar hallway looked! The central heating – how *warm* this Applecott House was. Like a hot bath, wonderful but also weirdly fake. The

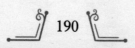

brightness of the electric lights, and how tacky and plasticky the tinsel suddenly seemed, after the dusky Victorian world. How *clean* it was! How colourful!

They sat up and looked at each other.

"That," said Ruby fervently, "was *amazing*. Not sure it's *quite* worth the Arctic conditions or the corsets and the sewing boxes. But that was *definitely* Christmas."

"What do you think happened to her?" said Alex. "To Edith, I mean? Do you think she was happy? Would Aunt Joanna know?"

"I doubt it," said Ruby, doubtfully. "The Victorians were ages ago."

"She'd be in the family tree anyway," said Alex. "Come on." And he jumped up and off towards the sitting room, where the photograph albums were kept.

The family tree was tucked into the back of one of these – a large, rather yellowy document, consisting of several sheets of A4 paper stuck together with ancient, crackly tape. Aunt Joanna had researched it herself, years ago, using census records and the local library and family things that had, one way and another, never left Applecott House. The Pilgrims were great collectors of weird and wonderful objects, and mostly really bad at throwing things away.

"We ought to take a photo or something of this," Ruby muttered. "It would make time-travelling a lot easier if we knew who everyone was supposed to be."

Alex didn't answer. He was following the thread of relations up the family tree. Aunt Joanna – Aunt Joanna's father – Aunt Joanna's grandfather –

"Ruby!" he said. "Look! Latimer Pilgrim's oldest son – look who he was! It's Uncle Edmund! Aunt Joanna's grandad!"

"No!" Ruby stared. But there it was in Aunt Joanna's curly handwriting. Latimer Pilgrim m. (that meant married) Louisa Pargitter. Edmund Pilgrim b. 1872 (b. meant born). "We should have known," she said. "Teddy *is* short for Edmund – at least, there's a boy in my class called Teddy and *he's* short for Edward, so I suppose it could just as easily be short for Edmund too."

"I thought Teddy was short for Theodore," said Alex, but he supposed he shouldn't be that surprised. Names were weird. There was a boy in *his* class at school who was called Alexander too, only *he* was Sascha for short.

"Imagine that baby being Aunt Joanna's grandad!" he said instead. "I thought the Victorians were ages and ages and ages ago!"

"Well, Aunt Joanna is quite old," said Ruby, but he could tell that she was shaken too. History was much closer to ordinary life than it ever seemed to be in school, despite the funny underwear.

"Is Edith on there?" he said. "Does it say what happened to her?"

They looked at the family tree. Edith Jane Pilgrim b. 1866.

"Blimey!" said Ruby. "Look at this!"

Alex stared at the entry.

"Well," he said. "She didn't die."

"She lived to eighty-four!" said Ruby. "And three husbands, wow! Hey, look, she was seventy-six when she married her last husband, that's pretty cool."

"But she looked so small and shy," said Alex.

"So?" said Ruby. "Small and shy women can get married too! And anyway, just because she was like that when she was little, doesn't mean she always was. What do you think happened to her? Do you think Aunt Joanna knows? Come on!"

She ran out of the room and into the kitchen, where Aunt Joanna was putting together welcome packs for the Christmas guests.

"Edith Pilgrim! Little girl who came over from India in Victorian times and lived with your – um

– great-great-grandparents' family. Do you know what happened to her?"

"Good heavens, Ruby!" Aunt Joanna put down the menu card and stared at her. "What are you blathering on about now?"

"She's on the family tree!" Ruby flapped the pieces of paper at Aunt Joanna, who visibly winced. "We just went back to—"

"Enough!" Aunt Joanna took the paper from Ruby and put it firmly on the table. "Where do you *get* all this family history from? Is it your dad? I never thought he was that interested."

"Dad's interested!" said Alex. "He—" Ruby elbowed him in the stomach.

"That *isn't* where we know about Edith from!"

she said. "We went back to 1873 and we met her! Her dad was going to put her in that horrible school Mum and Dad took us to last summer, but we persuaded them to keep her! Only, we wanted to know if he changed his mind."

"Goodness," said Aunt Joanna. "Now, do you think you could finish decorating the Christmas tree before you get sucked back to the stone age?"

"Aunt Joanna! Look, we can prove it! We've got Christmas stockings and everything!"

For a moment something flickered in Aunt Joanna's face – was it doubt? Belief? But almost instantly, it disappeared. She began exclaiming over the stocking and asking Ruby where she'd bought it from, and Ruby began protesting that

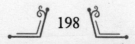

it was *real*, look, it was *Victorian*. The same old argument.

Alex wandered back into the hall and over to the mirror, rather wistful. They would go through it at least once more, Marian had proved that. But when? And why did this keep happening to them? They weren't particularly special. How long would it go on happening? For the rest of their lives?

As he stood there, wondering, the picture in the mirror changed. A woman in a golden ball gown appeared, her hair in an elaborate coiffure on the top of her head. She cocked her head to one side, as though appraising her reflection. Then she nodded to herself, satisfied, and disappeared.

Alex felt a thrill of mingled excitement and delight rush through him. A new adventure! And proof! Proof, at last that their story was real. He opened his mouth, to call to Aunt Joanna and Ruby to come and see. But before he could do so, the glass gave its familiar ripple. The picture vanished, and all was its ordinary self once more.

TAKE ANOTHER TRIP THROUGH TIME WITH ALEX AND RUBY!

CAN ALEX AND RUBY SOLVE A CRIME AND SAVE THE DAY?

CAN ALEX AND RUBY FIND A HOME FOR A LOST FRENCH ARISTOCRAT?

CAN ALEX AND RUBY SOLVE A RIDDLE AND UNCOVER A SECRET?